DIE A LITTLE

The only thing deadlier than a femme fatale ...
is two of them.

Lora King's brother Bill, a junior investigator with the District Attorney's office, meets a woman by chance and quickly marries her. Alice Steele is a beautiful and charming Hollywood wardrobe assistant, and although everyone else is entranced by her, Lora becomes suspicious of the inconsistencies in the stories from Alice's past. Intrigued, Lora decides to do some investigating of her own and it's not long before she's sucked into Hollywood's seedy underbelly, where she uncovers a shadowy world of drugs, prostitution and murder – and the deeper she digs, the more her own life begins to resemble Alice's sinister past ... and present.

DIE A LITTLE

DIE A LITTLE

by

Megan Abbott

Magna Large Print Books
Long Preston, North Yorkshire,
BD23 4ND, England.

British Library Cataloguing in Publication Data.

Abbott, Megan
    Die a little.

    A catalogue record of this book is
    available from the British Library

    ISBN   978-0-7505-3048-4

First published in Great Britain 2008 by Pocket Books UK
an imprint of Simon & Schuster UK Ltd.

Copyright © Megan Abbott, 2005

Cover illustration © Richard Fahey by arrangement with
Simon & Schuster UK Ltd.

The right of Megan Abbott to be identified as the author of this
work has been asserted in accordance with sections 77 and 78 of
the Copyright, Designs and Patents Act, 1988

Published in Large Print 2009 by arrangement with
Simon & Schuster UK Ltd.

Abbott, Megan E

Magna Large Pr Die a little / Magna Books Ltd.
    Megan Abbott

Printed and bou in Great Britain by
T.J. (Internation al) Ltd., Cornwall, PL28 3RW

LP

1856773

For Josh.

Acknowledgments

My warmest gratitude to Paul Cirone for all his efforts and conviction, and to Denise Roy for her keen editorial insight and sustaining guidance. To my early and encouraging readers and dear friends, Christine Wilkinson and Alison Levy. To Darcy Lockman, for her friendship and perpetual support. And without whom: Patricia and Philip Abbott, Joshua Abbott, Julie Nichols, Ralph and Janet Nase, and Jeff, Ruth, and Steven Nase. And most of all, to Joshua Gaylord.

Later, the things I would think about. Things like this: My brother never wore hats. When we were young, he wouldn't wear one even to church and my mother and then grandmother would force one on his head. As soon as he could he would tug it off with soft, furtive little boy fingers. They made his head hot, he would say. And he'd palm the hat and run his fingers through his downy blond hair and that would be the end of the hat.

When he began as a patrolman, he had to wear a cap on duty, but it seemed to him far less hot in California than in the South, and he bore up. After he became a junior investigator for the district attorney, he never wore a hat again. People often commented on it, but I was always glad. Seeing his bristly yellow hair, the same as when he was ten years old, it was a reminder that he still belonged to our family, no matter where we'd move or what new people came into our lives.

I used to cut my brother's hair in our kitchen every week. We would drink cola from the bottle and put on music and lay down newspapers, and I would walk around him in my apron and press my hand to his neck and forehead and trim away as he told

11

me about work, about the cases, about the other junior investigators and their stories. About the power-mad D.A. and his shiny-faced toadies. About the brave cops and the crooked ones. About all the witnesses, all his days spent trailing witnesses who always seemed like so much smoke dissolving into the rafters. His days filled with empty apartments, freshly extinguished cigarettes, radios still warm, curtains blowing through open windows, fire escapes still shuddering...

When I finished the cut, I'd hold out the gilt hand mirror from my mother's old vanity set and he would appraise the job. He never said anything but 'That's it, Sis,' or 'You're the best.' Sometimes, I would see a missed strand, or an uneven ledge over his ear, but he never would. It was always, 'Perfect, Sis. You've got the touch.'

Hours afterward, I would find slim, beaten gold bristles on my fingers, my arms, no matter how careful I was. I'd blow them off my fingertips, one by one.

For their honeymoon, just before New Year's 1954, my brother and his new wife went to Cuba for six days. It was Alice's idea. Bill happily agreed, though his first choice had been Niagara Falls, as was recommended by most of the other married couples we knew.

They came back floating on a cloud of their own beauty, their own gorgeous besottedness. It felt vaguely lewd even to look at them. They seemed to be all body. They seemed to be wearing their insides too close to the surface of their skin.

There is a picture of Alice. The photographer – I'm not sure who it was – was ostensibly taking a picture of our godparents, the Conrans, on their thirtieth wedding anniversary. But the photographer snapped too late, and Uncle Wendell and Aunt Norma are beginning to exit the frame with the embarrassed elation of those unused to such attention and eager to end it, and what you see instead is Alice's back.

She is wearing a demure black silk cocktail dress with a low-cut V in the back, and her alabaster skin is spread across the frame, pillowing out of the silk and curving sharply into her dark hair. The jut of her shoulder blades and the angular tilt of her cocked arm draw the eye irresistibly. So like Alice. She didn't even need to show her face or have a voice to demand complete attention.

It had all begun not six months before.

My chest felt flooded by my own heart. I could hardly speak, hardly breathe the whole way to the hospital, lights flashing over me, my mind careering. They said, 'What is your relation to William King?'

'What's wrong?'

'Are you his wife?'

'What's wrong with my brother?'

But he was fine. He was fine. I was running down the hospital corridor, shins aching from my heels hitting the floor so hard. I was running when I heard his voice echoing, laughing, saw his downy, taffy-colored hair, his handsome, stubby-nosed profile, his hand rubbing the back of his head as he sat on a gurney, smeary smile on his face.

'Lora.' He turned, speaking firmly to calm me, to strip the tight fear from my face. Hand out to grab my arm and stop me from plowing clear into him, he said, 'I'm fine. I just hit my head, got knocked out, but I'm fine.'

'Fine,' I repeated, as if to fix it.

His jacket over his arm, his collar askew, he had, I noted with a shiver, a break of browning blood on his shirt.

'Someone hit your car?'

'Nah. Nearly did, but I swerved out of the way. The driver kept going off the road and into a telephone pole. I stopped to help her, and while I was trying to get her out of her car, another car rear-ended it and knocked us both down. It was some show.'

He laughed when he said it, which was how I knew the driver was young and pretty, and troubling and helpless, all of which seemed, suddenly to me, to be just what he wanted, what he had been waiting for all along. It happened just like that. I realized it about him just like that, without ever having thought it before.

'Is she all right?'

'She had a concussion, but she's okay. She sprained her wrist trying to break her fall.' He touched his own wrist as he said it, with great delicacy. This gesture confirmed it all.

'Why did she veer off the road? What was wrong with her?'

'Wrong? I don't know. I never even...'

When the sergeant came by to get more details for his report, he told us that the woman, Alice Steele, would be released momentarily. I asked him if she had been drinking, and he said he didn't think so.

'No, definitely not. She was completely coherent,' my brother assured us both. The young sergeant respectfully nodded.

Her eyebrows, plucked and curvilinear like a movie star's, danced around as she spoke: My, how embarrassing – not just embarrassing but unforgivable – her actions were. She never should have been driving after taking a sedative even if it was *hours* before and never should have been driving on such a crowded road when she was so upset and crying over some complications in her life and with the rush to get to her friend Patsy's apartment because Patsy's boyfriend had hit her in the face with an ashtray. And, oh God, she wondered, what *had* happened to Patsy since she was never able to get there because of the accident. Would Patsy be all right? If there were scars, her modeling career would end in a heartbeat, and that would mean more trouble for Patsy, who'd had more than her share already.

Watching, listening, I imagined that this would be how this new woman in my brother's life would always talk, would always be. As it turned out, however, she rarely spoke so hazardously, so immoderately.

She had a small wound on her forehead, like a scarlet lip. It was this wound, I calculated, that had flowed onto my brother's shirtfront. A nurse was sewing stitches into it with long, sloping strokes the entire time she spoke to me.

I tried not to watch too closely as the wound transmuted from labial-soft and deep red to a thin, sharp, crosshatched line with only a trace of pucker. The nurse kept murmuring, 'Don't move, don't move,' as Alice gestured, twisting with every turn of phrase, never wincing, only offering an occasional squint at the inconvenience.

'Lora. Lora King,' I answered.

'You're the wife of my knight in shining armor?'

'No. The sister.'

'I'm Alice. Alice Steele. You're smiling.'

'No. Not at you.'

'Where is that heroic brother of yours, anyway? Don't tell me he's left?'

'No. He's here. He's waiting.'

A smile appeared quickly and then disappeared, as if she decided it gave away too much. As if she thought I didn't know.

The three of us in my sedan. I drove them to Bill's car, which was unharmed. I knew he would offer to drive her home and he did and they vanished into his sturdy Chevy like circling dangers. Patti Page trilled from the radio of his car as it drove off. I sat and listened until I couldn't hear it any longer. Then I drove home.

At first, it was the pretext of checking on her recovery.

Then, it was his friend Alice, who needed a ride to the studio, where she worked in the costume department as a seamstress's assistant. She lived with a girlfriend named Joan in a rooming house somewhere downtown.

Then, it was Alice, who had bought him the new tie he wore, with the thin periwinkle stripe.

17

Next, it was Alice, with whom he'd had chop suey because he happened to be by the studio around lunchtime.

At last, it was Alice over for dinner, wearing a gold blouse and heels and bringing a basket of pomegranates spiced with rum.

I prepared ham with pineapple rings and scalloped potatoes and a bowl of green beans with butter. Alice smoked through the whole meal, sipping elegantly from her glass and seeming to eat but never getting any closer to the bottom of her plate. She listened to my brother avidly, eyes shimmering, and complimented me on everything, her shoe dangling from her foot faintly but ceaselessly. It would be true in all the time I knew Alice that she would never, ever stop moving.

She asked many questions about our childhood, the different places we'd lived, our favorite homes, how we'd ended up in California and why we'd stayed. She asked me if I enjoyed teaching high school and how we'd found such a lovely house and if we liked living away from downtown Los Angeles. She asked me where I got my hair done and if I sewed and whether I enjoyed having a yard because she had 'always lived in apartments and had never had more than a potted plant and no green thumb besides, but who cares about that, tell me instead about how you keep such lovely petunias in this dry weather and does Bill help at all or

is he too busy playing cops and robbers,'
with a wink and blinding smile toward my
rapt brother.

Five months to the day after they met, they
decided to marry. The night they told me, I
remember there had been a tug over my eye
all day. A persistent twitch that wouldn't
give. Driving to the restaurant to meet
them, I feared the twitch would come at the
wrong moment and send me headlong into
oncoming traffic.

As I walked in, she was facing my freshly
shaved and bright-faced brother, who was all
shine and smile. I saw her shoulders rise like
a blooming heart out of an hourglass puce-
colored dress. He was towering over her, and
she was adjusting his pocket square with
dainty fingers. From the shimmer lining my
dear brother's face, from the tightness in his
eyes, I knew it was long over.

The day before they were married, we moved
Alice's things from the rooming house in
which she'd been living for over a year. It was
a large place in Bunker Hill, a house that had
once been very grand and now had turned
shaggy, with a bucket of sand for cigarettes at
the foot of its spiraling mahogany staircase.

Apparently, Bill had been trying to get her to move out since he first visited her there. 'I know places like this. I spend days knocking down the doors of places like this,' he had told her. 'It's no place for you.'

But, according to him, she only laughed and touched his arm and said that he should have seen her last place, in a bungalow court where, the first night she spent there, a man stabbed his girlfriend in the stomach with her knitting needle, or a fork, she couldn't remember which. 'She was all right,' Alice had assured him. 'It wasn't deep.'

When we helped her pack up, I noticed how many clothes Alice had, and how immaculately she kept them, soft sweaters nestled in stacks of plastic sleeves, hatboxes interlocked like puzzle pieces in the top of her closet, shoes in felt bags, heels stroked in cotton tufts to keep them from being scratched by the hanging shoe tree, dresses with pillowy skirts tamed by sweeping curls of tissue paper or shells of crinkly crepe.

Alice smiled warmly as I marveled at each glorious confection. She said she accumulated most of the clothes from her work at the studio. The seamstresses were often allowed to take cast-off garments deemed too damaged or too worn. No clothes or costumes were ever supposed to be given away but used over and over until the fabric dissolved like sugar. At a certain point, however, the clothes were passed to the girls, either because the designers could do nothing more with them, or as a favor or trade for extra or special work.

So after five years of studio work, Alice had accumulated quite an array of repaired clothes, the most glorious being a dress Claudette Colbert had worn, which was nearly impossible to put on or off. It was a delicate black velvet with netting around the neck, and it made Alice's small chest look positively architectural, like cream alabaster jutting up from her wasp waist.

Our godparents hosted the wedding party after the ceremony at City Hall. The other junior investigators from the D.A.'s office and my fellow teachers from Westridge School for Girls filled the small house.

No one came from Alice's family. Her only guests were a few coworkers from the studio, who sat on a corner couch, smoking and straightening their stockings.

At the time, she said that she had no family to invite, that she was orphaned and alone. She was a native Southern Californian, if there was such a thing. She was born in Santa Monica Hospital to a domestic with Hollywood aspirations and a recently discharged chauffeur. That was all we really knew.

At the party, my eyes could barely leave

her, this woman who had entered our life and planted herself so firmly at its sharp center.

She buzzed around the party, hovering with large, rain pail eyes, a body compact, pulled taut over every angle, raw-boned, and a few years or a few ounces away from gaunt, ghostly. Her appeal was a kind of thrilling nervous energy, a railrack laugh that split her face in gleaming abandon.

There was a glamour to her, in her unconventional beauty, in her faintly red-rimmed eyes and the bristly, inky lashes sparking out of them, blinking incessantly, anxiously. Her hair was always perfectly coiffed, always shining and engineered, her lips artfully painted magenta. When she'd turn that black-haired head of hers, a collarbone would pop out disturbingly. She had no curves. She was barely a woman at all, and yet she seemed hopelessly feminine, from her airy walk, her muzzy, bobbing gesticulations, her pointy-toed shoes, and the spangly costume jewelry dangling from her delicate wrists.

Even though Bill and Alice repeatedly urged me to live with them, I moved into a small apartment while they honeymooned.

'I can't imagine you two apart. What is Bill

without Lora? Lora without Bill?' Alice would say, dark eyes pounding.

'I'll be closer to school. It'll be easier,' I assured them, packing up the chocolate-colored figured rug, white and rose chairs, and rough cream drapes of our living room, the heavy dining room table we'd had since children, the blond bedroom set my grand-parents had given me upon my graduating teachers' college.

I moved to a one-bedroom on Pasadena's west side, as Bill and Alice prepared to move from our duplex to a pretty new ranch house in tonier South Pasadena. They bought it with Bill's savings, borrowing against his pension.

It was strange at first. Bill and I had lived together for so long, not just as children but always. As I polished the dining room set, wedged uncomfortably in the corner of the living room of my new apartment, I remem-bered a thousand evenings spent at the round, knotty table, long nights when I was studying for my certification and Bill was at the police academy. He always wanted to work for the district attorney. He wasn't joining the force because it was in the family (it wasn't), like so many of the others, and he wasn't doing it because he wanted to see action, to be a tough guy. He did it out of a larger purpose that he would never say outright but that I could feel in everything he said, every look he gave as we drove through the city, as we saw the things one can see in a city, driving through, watching, watching everything.

Now, rubbing a soft cloth over each knot in the table, I could nearly picture us seated there, books spread out, coffeepot warm. He would rub his eyes, run a finger under his collar, sometimes pass me a grin like 'Lora, look at us, look how devoted we are, look how alike we are, we're the same, really.'

And we were. Taking notes, furrowing our brows, our necks curled, craned, sore, and aching, and yet exhilarated, our whole lives beginning and everything waiting for us.

Before my brother met Alice, there were always women telling me, 'I can't believe your brother's not married' or 'How is it no woman has snatched him up yet?' I never really knew how to answer.

He could have married anyone.

And he had girlfriends, but it never really led anywhere. When I first started teaching, he dated Margie Reichert, the sister of his partner. Tiny with fluffy hair and empty eyes, Margie had the vaguely tubercular look of a child-woman. She often ran into minor troubles generally instigated by her shyness, her difficulty in speaking up before it was too late. When Bill discovered Margie was paying for utilities on her small apartment, in violation of her lease, he spoke with the landlord and ensured Margie receive a refund for the months of bills she'd paid. When Margie's boss at Rush's Department Store fired her for stealing, Bill quickly learned the other salesgirls were using Margie to conceal their own shortchanging. Soon enough, Margie had her job back.

Everyone was certain they would marry.

Somehow, they never did. The time came and passed, and they seemed to see each other less, and Margie decided to move with her family to San Diego after all. There seemed no pressing reason to stay.

Besides, Bill was so absorbed in his job, in getting to where he wanted to go. And we were this team, both moving forward, digging our feet in, making roots. A new family, a family born anew.

In this fashion, six years had passed.

And now, it was as it should be. Bill had found someone. It seemed, at some point, I would, too.

Let me say this about my brother. My brother, he was one of those gleaming men, a jaw sharp, color always flushing up his straightedge cheekbones. And, amid all the masculine rigidity, all the razor lines and controlled flesh, lay a pair of plushy, girlish lips, pouty and pink, and a pair of lovely and nearly endless eyelashes – eyelashes so extravagant that as a young boy he had taken our mother's nail scissors to them. But of course they'd grown back, immutable.

With a more moneyed background you could imagine him as one of those glorious, arrogant, seersucker-suited men out of novels. But with his middlebrow roots, he could never be less than earnest, more than provincial in his views, his tastes.

And yet, there was Alice.

While they lounged in a haze of lovesick in Cuba, a honeymoon far beyond my brother's modest income, their new bungalow filled itself happily, riotously – gifts from family and friends, but also things Alice ordered to set up their new home.

A full set of smooth pink and gray Russel Wright everyday dinnerware, my mother's Haviland china in English Rose, a series of copper fish Jell-O molds, a large twelve-slice chrome toaster, a nest of Pyrex mixing bowls, a gleaming bar set, tumblers, old-fashioneds, and martini glasses with gold-leaf diamonds studding the rims, a bedroom set with soft, dove gray silk quilted coverlets, matching lamps with dove gray porcelain gazelles as their bases, a vanity with a round mirror and a silver deco base, a delicate stool of wrought curlicues holding up a pale peach heart seat cushion, a tightly stuffed and sleekly lined sofa, love seat, and leather wing chairs in the living room, with its green trim, jungle-patterned curtains, and a large brass cage in which a parrot named Bluebeard lived.

The only remnants of our old house, aside from the china and a family desk of plantation oak, are a set of rose-hued photographs, one of Bill and me at ages six and nine, and one of us with our parents in front of a fireplace before their last Christmas, before dying in a base-camp fire overseas, my father in plaid robe and Santa hat perched jauntily, Joel McCrea – handsome, and my mother, all ripe grin and tight curls, tugging us close to her lace-trimmed dress.

Bill and I are so unmistakably siblings, both with rough blond hair, popping eyes, and downy faces, round elbows curling out of matching holiday suspenders. While mine attached to a stiff skirt and Bill's to short pants, our seated poses conceal the distinction.

When I first visit the newlyweds' house, I can't help but notice there are no framed family photos from Alice's side, not even a stray snapshot. When I ask her why, she says she doesn't have any. Thinking about it, however, she remembers one bit of history she can show me. Running to her closet and back, she brings out an old Culver City newspaper article that ran in honor of the fiftieth anniversary of an establishment called Breuer's Chocolates. Accompanying the story is a photo of a shapely young girl in her teens, a blur of black hair and arms with curlicue dimples, sales smock pulled tightly across her chest, a cloud of airy divinity puffs in front of her.

'That's me, believe it or not.' Alice smiles. Finger pressed to the round girl in the picture, she talks about how she used to have a soft white belly, sweetly spreading pale thighs, a faint, faint pocket of lush flesh under her chin. It happened when she was working at Breuer's, making a dollar a day.

As Alice tells it, she would come to work so hungry, having eaten only eggs and hash for dinner the night before. How, after all, could she stand it, inhaling that rich, warm smell all day and not sampling it? It was easier to filch a whole box from the wrapping room than to slip them out individually from the case. All day long, she would make trips to the ladies' room or her locker and savor a piece or two, a waxy cream, a brittle honeyed toffee, a dissolving coconut spume.

Of course, she eventually tired of chocolate, but not for a long time, and when she did, there were nougats, jellied candies shaped like wedges of lemon or lime, butterscotch coins she could slide under her tongue all day, paper sacks of sharp candy corns. Oh, she wouldn't be hungry until late at night after a full day at the store. And then a smooth hard-boiled egg or a starchy wedge of day-old was all she needed. A dentist later told her she was lucky to have teeth like a hillbilly, impenetrable.

As I look at the woolly image, she explains how, when she left the chocolate shop for a sewing factory, she lost fifteen pounds in a month, both from working hard, long hours and from nights out with her new girlfriends – other factory girls who brought Alice into their circle, spending nights at the army canteen, dancing and drinking gin fizzes instead of eating dinner and sleeping.

Looking at the younger Alice, however, I'm struck by something. It is clearly her in the picture: her thick eyelashes, upturned nose, wide mouth. But there is something in her face that seems utterly foreign, utterly exotic and strange to me. Like someone I've never met, someone who no longer is.

It is one month after the wedding and long past midnight, and I am lying in bed in my brother's new house, wide awake, thinking I should have made the drive home, where I could have nursed my insomnia with some exams I needed to grade, or at least played the radio or turntable to ease my racing mind. Instead, I am holed up in the make-shift sewing room/guest bedroom, staring at the alarming seamstress dummy lurking out of the darkness. I wonder how early in the morning I can leave without being rude.

Somewhere beyond the door, I hear a faint rustling, and I imagine my brother awake. We would have a late-night talk, chamomile tea or even a cold beer, me curled in a chair and him slouched on the floor, rubbing my feet. We would play records, and he would talk through the case that was bothering him, or I would talk about the student who was troubling me, and the night would curl in on itself so comfortably.

I hear what sounds like pages turning. Someone is definitely up, and it must be my brother. Alice's fourth martini has to have put her in a very sound sleep.

I slide my robe on and make my way to the door. Opening it delicately, and walking down the hall, I see one of the living room lights on. As I move closer, I realize it is only Alice after all. Her legs tucked beneath her on a wing chair, she is paging through one of our thick old family photo albums.

I am about to turn around and head back, not wanting to disturb her, but as I do, my eyes play a funny trick.

I stop suddenly at the archway and find myself stifling a tight gasp. Under the harsh lamp, in sharp contrast to the dark room, her eyes look strangely eaten through. The eyes of a death mask, rotting behind the gleaming facade. A trick of the light some-how—

'Lora!' Alice says, surprised, jolting me out of my thoughts. She realizes how loudly she's said my name and covers her mouth with her hand, smiling. 'You scared me.'

'I'm sorry,' I say. 'I couldn't sleep.'

'Ditto. Sit down.'

I move over to the sofa beside her, tightening the belt on my robe and trying to avoid looking her straight in the eyes, which still have that rotting look, set deeper than her doll-like face.

'I was just looking at some of the old King family history,' she whispers with a tone of playful conspiracy.

'Really?' I look over at the pages open in her lap. There are my brother and I fishing on the dock of our grandparents' property, he waving a mangy trout in the air. We were probably around four and seven, and both of us tanned and naked to the waist in a way that makes me blush.

'The faces alone – if it weren't for those little braids tucked behind your ears, I couldn't tell you two apart,' Alice says, trying to meet my gaze.

'Yes. Same blond curls, until Dad made Bill get regular military-style cuts.'

'And you a little tomboy, too.'

'We both liked to fish and play outdoors. Cowboys and Indians, I guess. I don't really remember,' I say, even as I remember everything, *even in one wave of sharp grass, rowboat creek, feet pounding tag, whispers from top bunk to bottom in the heavy July night.*

'It feels so different, so ... impossibly different from my childhood.' Alice rubs her brow.

'I guess you were a city girl.'

'Hmmm,' she murmurs. 'That, too. And no brothers or sisters and no grandparents I ever met. And no homestead. I mean, I know you moved a lot because of your father's different posts, but it seems like you always had a real home. A house, the same furniture and things. We always lived in furnished places. I remember instead of counting sheep, I used to recite the places I'd lived: five bungalow courts' – she counted them off on her fingers –'Corrington Arms, El Cielo Court, La Alambra Bungalows, La Cienega Arms, Golden Dreams Bungalows. And eight hotels, four rented rooms, two in-house maid's quarters, and one rented house that my mother skipped out on so fast we left everything behind but a laundry bag full of dirty clothes. We never even had the same car for more than a few months.'

Alice grins, as if suddenly remembering. 'The only thing that was constant was the set of Johnson Brothers china my father had from his mother and her mother. It dated back to the Gold Rush, I think. When I was little it had twelve place settings. Each move, when my father would pack it up carefully in the same old cloth napkins, there would be fewer pieces. I broke a few washing them. Rough moves broke lots of cups, especially the handles. But mostly my mother would throw plates or saucers at my father when they fought. Surest way to get a reaction out of him.'

I smile and feel relieved to see Alice's eyes turn gray-brown, like coffee with cream. It is a story filled with dirty ghosts, yet there's a fondness in the way she tells it, a pleasure in its rangy tumult.

'I always used to sweep up the shards afterward. I can picture the little blue flowers now. One night...

'One night, she was so mad, so furious, I remember she cracked one over her own head. And I remember laughing, because it was funny, like in a movie. Like Laurel and Hardy or something. But then it didn't seem funny at all when I looked at her face, which looked cracked, too. There was blood, yes, but it wasn't that. Her face was so ... unhinged ... that it was as if it had split. As if she had split.' Alice touches her face as she says it, the heel of one hand under her chin, the other on her forehead. 'It scared me. My pop, too. He kept looking at her. She was standing still, her arm hanging there, holding the broken shard at her side. She was shaking, but she didn't say anything. Like she was shocked by what she'd done. Like she couldn't believe she'd gone that far.'

As Alice tells me this, I turn away from her. I stare hard at my hands, wrung around each other. I am afraid to look over at her because I know what I will see. I will see her eyes turning, always turning back to rot.

After the honeymoon period, when real life had to resume for them, Alice was determined to make a home. She had quit her job, had her last day at the studio just before the wedding. She was so relieved, had found herself disgusted by her work, tearing fabric apart and replacing panels because of a variety of stains left by actresses, stains suggesting encounters had while still in costume. She'd throw them in the bin to be laundered, always asking the laundry girls never to bring her costumes that hadn't gone through them first. She wouldn't miss that, she assured me. Not one bit.

Now, hunched over her Singer, she made curtains for every room, bright curtains that, hung stiffly or blew languorously; she painted the walls by hand, apple green, buttercup yellow, crème caramel. She planted tomatoes in one corner of the small yard and dug flower bulbs along the perimeter, trimming the grass around every curve of the small footpath to the front door.

Bill insisted I take all our cooking and baking wares, farm-style pieces of cast iron and heavy wood. It was just as well for Alice, who wanted her own things, and she set out to fit her sunny yellow-painted kitchen with all things modern.

Small, well-chosen pieces, of course. She bought a set of casserole dishes with rattan frames made by Gladding, McBean. She asked my brother for, and received, Broil King by the Peerless Electric Company for her birthday. She bargained successfully with the salesmen at McCreary's Department Store in downtown Pasadena for a prime deal on a set of Samson folding chairs by Shwayder Brothers. She bought a Cornwall Thermo Tray with gold finish and wooden handles for serving hot artichoke hors d'oeuvres and tuna squares.

Only a few times would I actually see Alice cleaning, but the immaculate house revealed that cleaning must have been going on all the time. I could picture her on hands and knees, hair covered in a topknot cloth, scrubbing fervently, greedily, so gladly because nothing seemed to make her happier than seeing pure lines, smooth surfaces, sharp corners, and the smell always of cleanliness, intense, pungent, shaded over with the scent of fresh-cut flowers or a simmering stovetop.

Despite all her prewedding glamour, Alice quickly became the most quiet, the most demure of a quiet and demure set of junior investigators' wives. She was the first to bring the tuna noodle casserole to the new family that moved in, or to the household with the sick mother. She attended church with Bill and often me, turning the pages of the hymnal with her immaculate white gloves, apologizing that her half-Catholic, half-Pentecostal upbringing hadn't prepared her for the Lutheran service we attended.

Almost instantaneously it seemed, Alice, with her fresh and lovely looks and her handsome, upstanding husband, had made friends in the neighborhood. It was not long before she and the other women in the cul-de-sac began buying each other things, visiting gifts, housewarmings. They bought each other mint julep sets made of aluminum and cork, copper fruit bowls, tidbit stands, pink Polynesian chop plates adorned with a black palm frond pattern, spun aluminum nesting bowls with neat reed handles, Pyrex hostess sets for picnics on the back lawns, Klise Frosted Oak relish boats and cheese boards with Lucite inserts, Manta Ray centerpiece bowls with a chic black glaze or elegant figured white, canapé rosettes with three banked levels which as the pretty box said, 'make this tray an ideal serving accessory for 'after bridge' and for afternoon teas.'

For months, it seemed all she did was bake. She was learning by doing, with Betty Crocker perched on the counter, with *Joy of Cooking,* with our mother's dog-eared collection of country cookbooks. She made a raspberry-coconut jelly roll for a brunch with the Leders and Conlans. A rum-and-cherry-cola marble cake for a cocktail party. Caramel-apple chiffon cupcakes soaked through with Dry Sack cream sherry for the Halloween party. On Bill's birthday, she spent hours making cream-puff swans shaped from what she carefully pronounced as a 'pâté à chou.' For a block party, almond icebox cake and cornflake macaroons. Chow mein – noodle haystacks and fried spaghetti cookies for a neighborhood association bake sale. For a dinner party, white chocolate grasshopper pie still foaming with melted marshmallows and doused with Hiram Walker. More dinner parties and still racier items, ambrosia brimming with Grand Marnier, a fruit-cocktail gelatin ring nearly a foot high and glistening. As the parties grew more elaborate, more frenetic, bourbon balls studded with pecans and Nesselrode pie with sweet Marsala and chestnuts. Strawberries Biltmore covered with vanilla custard sauce. Baked Alaska drizzled through with white rum. Peach Melba suffused with framboise.

Soon, she had no rival. In the neighborhood and among the investigators' wives, she set all the trends, and everyone else followed.

It was as though she had waited her whole life for this.

As the months passed, however, I began to see glimpses, odd, awry glimpses of a different Alice, an Alice somewhere between the girl in the picture of Breuer's Chocolates and this matchless homemaker. At parties or bridge gatherings, in the ladies' room after three stingers, she'd lean over to me, hot alcohol and perfume, and whisper something like a clue, 'When I was a department store model, a customer once paid me seventy-five dollars to come home with her and put on her dead husband's clothes, piece by piece. She played 'I'm Forever Blowing Bubbles' on her turntable over and over all night. She never laid a hand on me, but she might have. Love is funny, isn't it?'

Or 'This old roommate of mine, Lois, she bathed every night in rubbing alcohol. She'd bathe in it for hours, and then come out and coat, *coat* her body in jasmine lotion –

together, the smell was like a punch in the face.

'Then – listen, Lora – then, one night, my other roommate, Paulette, had a date over and he – his name was Dickie – was on the fire escape smoking. Next thing we hear this scream, horrible, like an animal under a car. Apparently, Dickie had thrown his lit cigarette down the alley and the wind carried it up and through the bathroom window. Lois was just getting out of the bath covered with the alcohol. We ran in, and we got the bath mat around her, rolled her on the floor, like they tell you to do in school.

'Her skin felt like crinkled paper. I could barely look at her. I kept thinking her flesh was going to fall off in my hands. Then it turned soft and shiny, like wax. The bath mat was cheap, and bits of it stuck to her. When Paulette looked down and saw what was happening, she started screaming. I had to slap her three times.

'Lois was okay, some second-degree burns on her stomach and her thighs. What was funny was that Dickie felt so bad, he kept visiting her at the hospital, and the next thing you know, they were a couple. Things happen like that sometimes. It didn't last, those things seldom do, but when I would see them, out in Santa Monica or Hollywood or something, they'd be sitting together, smoking like chimneys, and I would laugh, and

Lois, one tough nut, she'd laugh back and wink and say, 'Where there's smoke there's fire, honey.'"

It is after one of Alice's triumphal dinner parties. Alice and I are washing dishes while Bill drives a few intoxicated guests home. As she leans her face over the steam rising from the scalding dishwater she favors ('Splendid for the complexion'), we laugh about how enamored of Bill his senior coworkers seem.

'I guess they're especially glad they have someone young enough not only to run after witnesses but also to play first-string quarterback for them against Glendale PD.'

'He's the youngest by six years.' I smile, trying to be careful drying Alice's new china. 'The second youngest junior investigator ever to work in the D.A.'s office.'

'I didn't know that. How did he get such a position so young?' Alice turns and looks at me, face piping red and dappled, eyes lit.

'You mean he never told you?' I say. Then, shaking my head, 'That's so like him.'

'Never told me what?'

It is then that I tell her how Bill was promoted after an incident that received a great deal of local attention.

It was his fourth year on the force, and Bill's partner had just retired. A rookie officer named Lester was assigned to him. Only a few months out of the academy, Lester was thrilled to have such a hot beat.

The first night they rode together, they received a call from a fiercely angry woman who claimed her teenage son was spending time with a street gang and probably had been involved in recent vandalism and maybe even the latest stickup in the neighborhood. He had been a good, churchgoing boy, and now he was on his way to being a hoodlum, plain and simple. It was all on account of this *pachuca* girl he had fallen for who had been to reform school and only dated boys who proved their street mettle.

Bill and Lester went over to her apartment, which was heavy with die-cut crosses on the walls and a plaster saint in one corner. Bill was dubious. The woman, tightly wound and incessantly gesturing with the large tinted photograph of her son at age four in her hand, seemed unreliable and maybe even a little crazy. Bill started to wonder whether or not her son was still even in the picture. Maybe he had run away; he'd seen lots of things like that, lonely-sad or lonely-mad people worried about or seeking revenge against spouses, friends, lovers who were actually long gone.

The woman decided, tossing the photograph on the worn couch, that Bill and Lester should help her search her son's things for evidence of criminal activity. Aching for action, Lester started up to his feet, assuring her that they would find something, if there were something to find.

Bill couldn't get over his doubts, and watching the woman tugging at the hem of her cotton shift dress over and over and bemoaning her fate to have such a rotten son with her own blood, *her own blood* running through his veins, he paused a long second before following Lester toward the bedroom.

The small room was immaculate. Not a boy's room at all, Bill thought, still working on his theory that this boy had beat town months, years before, or had been killed in Korea or maybe died before he'd reached adolescence. He'd seen stranger, after all.

The twin bed was tidily made. A chair against one wall had a football resting on it. A snapshot of a pretty girl with a scarf sat on the dresser top, along with a small trophy. As Lester bent down to look under the bed, Bill moved to the trophy out of curiosity. He was thinking, This doesn't look like a sports trophy, more like a–

It was at this moment that the closet door slammed open with a deadly clap and a boy of about fifteen stormed out with a thick Louisville Slugger in both hands. Before Bill could get his gun, the boy was on him, pounding. They both fell to the floor with a thud, and the mother was screaming in horror as Bill shouted to Lester, 'Shoot him, shoot him,' with the blows coming straight to his head. He could feel his skull cracking, denting like a melon before everything went blurry, then black.

In what was actually only a few seconds later, Bill's eyes shot open just as the bat was about to come straight down on his head. He found himself shooting, and the boy fell backward, like a duck in a shooting gallery. The mother, apparently just as surprised as Bill, that her son was in the apartment, fainted in grand style. Fighting to keep conscious, Bill managed to radio for backup right before he passed out again.

It turned out that Lester had panicked. When the boy began pummeling Bill, he ran out of the apartment, and they found him several blocks away, hiding in an alley.

Bill was in the hospital for two weeks with a fractured skull, dislocated shoulder, and lacerations on his face and chest.

The boy was seriously wounded but not killed. Bill, even in his half-conscious state, had managed to hit him in the shoulder to disable him.

After he was discharged from the hospital, Bill was honored by the chief of police. His attacker turned out to have been involved in the murder of another officer earlier that day, and Bill became a minor hero, which enabled his dreamed-for reassignment to the prosecutor's office, unheard of for a twenty-seven-year-old.

I tell Alice all of this, and she is silent, washing slowly, eyes focused, mascara dewy, flecked. She listens as I try to tell her in a way to make her understand, understand everything. I know the way I tell it is everything: There is so much to know about my brother. Some things she might already understand, some things she should, she must recognize. When I finish, she looks at me with an expression heavy with meaning, about what she now knows about her husband and somehow, somehow what she now seems to think she knows about me.

Suddenly, we are jolted out of the moment by a knock on the kitchen door. I walk over to the window, expecting to see a partygoer returning for a forgotten coat. Instead, it is a tiny, dark-haired girl who looks about sixteen.

'Neighbor?' I ask, beckoning Alice.

Alice looks past my shoulder. When she does, I see something pass over her face quickly but unmistakably.

Recovering quickly, she assembles a smile of happy surprise at the intrusion and, nearly tumbling into the dish rack, moves past me to open the door.

'Lois.' She waves the girl in, wiping her hands on her apron. 'Come in. Um, Lora, there's someone I'd like you to meet.'

With a sharp red grin, the girl enters. Closer now, I can see she is older than she first appeared, perhaps in her mid-twenties. And, as if in some slapstick silent movie about a misbehaving wife, she wears an unmistakable black eye.

'Hi, honey,' she hums with a vaguely southern intonation.

'Got a steak?'

'Lois, Lora. Lora, Lois,' Alice says tightly as she opens the refrigerator. Alice, being Alice, does have a steak on hand. She hands it to Lois, who slaps it across her cheek and slumps down at the kitchen table.

Not sure what to make of the scene, I mentally reject a series of things to say. Each one sounds ridiculous, given the circumstances. It is at this point that I remember Alice's story about her friend Lois: *Where there's smoke there's fire.*

As I try to find my voice, I notice a starburst of broken blood vessels between Lois's lid and temple.

'I got socked,' she burbles, smiling lazily under the steak.

'I didn't mean to–'

'It's okay. I'd stare, too. It's a peach.' She doesn't move as she speaks, as if determined

45

not to let the steak budge an inch. As if doing so might allow her face to fall off.

'Lois is a friend from the studios. She's an actress.'

'I'm an actress, all right,' Lois slurs, staring straight at me with a sad smile.

'In pictures?'

'That's right.'

'Have you been in any I might know?'

'You can see me jerk a soda next to Dana Andrews in one. In another, I wave a big peacock feather over Maria Montez. And if I knew how to swim, I'd be wearing a tiara in a tank right now over at MGM in the new Esther Williams picture.'

'That's great,' I say. 'I mean, so many actresses can't get any work.'

'They don't know the right people,' she replies, still smiling. Alice looks at her, turning the water off at the sink.

'I guess it's connections along with the talent,' I say, removing my apron. 'And luck.'

'Lois makes her own luck,' Alice says.

I turn to Lois, who looks back at me with a wink.

One Sunday, I receive a message from my building manager that Alice called while I was out and is desperate for me to come over.

When I arrive, feeling a twinge of trepidation, what I find is both less and more worrying.

There are huge platters of food everywhere – on the large Formica table, leaves out, on the kitchen counters, on the seats of the chairs, even on the top of the refrigerator and the windowsills. Round plates of deviled eggs, quivering tomato aspic, large glass bowls of seven-layer salad, smudgy glass tureens of trifle, copper molds filled with fruit-studded Jell-O – where is the suckling pig, I wonder. And then Alice amid all this, hair pulled tightly back, flushed almost obscenely, glassy sheen of sweat on her face, neck, collarbones. The radio, teetering precariously on the windowsill next to a dish of creamed spinach with bacon, blares jazzy Cuban love songs. Her eyes, my God, her eyes are very nearly radiating, blinking spasmodically, pupils pulsing.

'It's a surprise party, Lora! A party for our darling, our Bill.'

I gather my breath. 'What's the occasion?'

'I had this revelation, Lora.' She tears out at me, smile like a pulled rubber band. 'You don't even know. I woke up with it. He works so hard. And that story you told me. Oh my God.'

She clutches her hand to her chest before continuing. 'He carries this crazy city on his shoulders, and what does he get? We take him for granted. Well, *I* do. Look at what he does, each and every day.

'This is for him, Lora. I just leaped out of bed and headed for the grocery store. I still had my slippers on, Lora. The store manager followed me around the whole time. He was afraid I might fall. He carried my groceries to the car. I've been cooking, baking all day. All day. I hope Bill doesn't get home before it's all finished.

'I need you, Lora. I need you to hang those decorations in the bags over there. And make the phone calls.

'We need to hang the lights, arrange the tiki torches, pass out the ashtrays, the bamboo coasters I bought. These wonderful coconut tumblers that I'll fill with daiquiri. Can you make daiquiris, Lora? I don't know how, but I bought ten pounds of ice.

She can't stop moving, stop talking. She is like a windup toy, or dominoes falling, unstoppable.

At no point do I stop and ask Alice anything. I just put on my apron. There doesn't seem to be anything I can say to stop her. I don't know what I *would* say. So, within a few minutes of first seeing the spectacle, I am hanging palm fronds from streamers to the sound of ukulele music, listening to Alice make phone call after phone call, her voice pressed and hot.

Somehow, somehow – for Alice alone could make something like this work – it all comes together, and by the time my brother comes home, wide-eyed and weary, Alice's whirring energy melds seamlessly with the larger excitement of a group of neighbors and a handful of fellow teachers and my godparents, all swept up in Alice's frenzy and heads bobbing under pulsing tiki lights and the purple and red luminescence of dozens of bright lanterns.

And all of them, everyone she invites, show up. And they all eat and they dance and they toast Bill as if they had actually started that day thinking of what they might say about his hard work and strong character. And Bill keeps looking around dazedly, not knowing what to say, biting his lower lip and spinning slightly, plate sagging in his hand, dripping pineapple glaze on the patio, too stunned to lift his wrist and steady himself.

As Alice drags out a tub of firecrackers to the delight of the crowd, I sidle up beside him. He looks down at me, putting a drowsy arm around my shoulder, his finger tickling my ear. We stand there, without saying anything, watching Alice dart around like a firefly. It seems like we are both thinking the same thing. Or at least, what I am thinking in full, he is wondering in part. *How long can this go on? This fever pitch, this spinning, quaking thing before us. Forever or a little less?*

And then, so soon after it might have been the following week...

'But, Bill, you're telling me Alice is qualified to teach high school?'

'She is. I mean, she's qualified to teach home economics. She studied it. At Van Nuys Community College.' He's followed me into my car after lunch, sits down next to me on the bench seat.

'Well, she'd have to get her teaching certificate.' I shrug. 'It takes months of coursework and student teaching.' I wonder if Bill's sudden urgency has anything to do with the surprise party.

'No, no. She has her teaching certificate. She got it to teach in Lomita about four years ago. But then she finally got in the seamstresses' union and started working for the studios instead.'

'Really? Well, that's great, Bill,' I say, meaning it, really meaning it. Alice content means Bill content, after all.

And anyone could see Alice was desperate

to channel her energy into a new project. 'Long afternoons,' she'd say to me, eyes a little too bright, neck a little too straight, teeth a little on edge, 'the afternoons, Lora, are *endless.*'

'So do you think you could talk to Don Evans? Maybe offer to bring her in so he could meet her? I'm sure if they met her, they'd see she'd be a great addition. I'm sure she'd charm the pants off them. And the kids would love her.'

'But I'm not sure what I say means much. For hiring, especially. I'm not senior faculty.'

'But you'll try?' He looks down at me, squeezing my fingers gently.

'She's my sister now, isn't she?' I smiled.

As it happens, it is all too easy. Principal Evans is eager to make a quick hire, with Miss Lincoln ready to leave and begin planning her wedding. It seems like the whole process unfolds effortlessly, with Alice coming for an interview and receiving a modest offer two days later, contingent on her submitting appropriate credentials. Within three weeks, she will be in the classroom.

'Tell me everything about these girls, Lora,' she says, the table in front of her papered with open books *(Mrs Lovell's First Book of Sewing, Teaching Domestic Arts to the Young, The National Association of Home Economics Teachers Presents a Guide for Lesson Plans),* pads of paper, notes, an oversize calendar filed with notations like 'Begin pillowcase' and Basting work.' Two pencils poked out of her upswept hair.

'What do you want to know?'

'Anything. I don't even know what to ask. What do I say? Will they do what I ask them to?'

'You taught before, to get your certificate. Just do what you did then.'

'But these girls … are they very … what are they like?'

'They're just girls. They do what they're told. Just don't let them get the better of you. You know, passing notes, talking behind their hands to each other during class.'

'I'm going to start with a simple project: napkin. Then a pillowcase. We'll work up to grander things: an evening jacket with shirring.'

I bite my lip. 'That's fine, Alice. But I don't think you can have fourteen- or fifteen-year-olds make evening jackets. They're not spending their time at nightclubs.'

Alice looks up at me, eyes wide. 'No, no, of course not. But they might wear it to a dance. They go to dances, after all, don't they?'

'Yes, but these girls aren't as … sophisticated as the ones in Los Angeles. They're small town girls, really. What if you made a nice flounced skirt instead?'

'Is that what Miss Lincoln had them make?'

'No. No, I think they made middy blouses or jumpers.'

Alice looks down at her calendar, hands shaking slightly. 'You think I'm a fool.' She smiles weakly.

'Of course not, Alice.' I lean forward, toward her. 'You're going to be fine.'

'They'll love me,' Alice says, looking up at me for a moment, then back down at her lesson plan decisively. 'You'll see. They'll absolutely love me.'

It is all as Alice predicts. She begins teaching and everything proceeds fluently. It strikes me that a focus for Alice's queer restlessness was all she had needed: just apply the same fervor to teaching that she had to the house, to being a new wife.

The girls are intimidated by her, not surprisingly. The intimidation that comes with intense infatuation. Even Nonny Carlyle, the most popular girl in school, settles in her seat, focused on the sewing machine, listening closely as Alice explains the different stitches, how to thread the new machines.

Alice wears her hair in straight-cut bangs, and within a week Aileen Dobrowski, Linda Fekete, Mary Carver, even Nonny Carlyle herself all come to school with freshly shorn bangs. They stay after class, circling Alice's desk, showing her pictures in magazines, in *Vogue* and *Cineplay* and *Screenstar,* pictures of dresses they want Alice to look at, ideas they want her opinion about. Alice, eyes jumping, is only too glad to indulge them, although her interest runs on an egg timer and it is never too long before she smiles and tells them they can discuss it more tomorrow; she has a husband to get to, a pot roast to make, a house to clean.

Each day, we drive home together, chatting about each classroom interaction, each charming or charmless student comment. Still, it is only a few weeks when the rush of the performance, the velocity of daily events, seem already to have worn off. I guess I am surprised at how quickly things turn. While she doesn't say so, it's clear that the pleasures have waned. She still talks ceaselessly, but no longer about school, about anything but school. When she settles in the car at the end of the day, her whole body seems deflated, like she has peeled herself out of some awful costume and tossed it aside.

At Bill's encouragement, Alice and I begin going out for 'girls' nights' once a month. Nights that are at least as much about getting ready – radio moaning, hair spray buffering the air, Alice with needle and thread fitting me into new dresses she's made from studio-scrapped gossamer – as they are about the destination.

Having Alice in our life makes me think of what it might have been like to have sisters or close girlfriends. Here we are in our slips and stockings, laughing and running around, cigarettes dangling (only with Alice do I smoke) as we try to get ready. Alice plucks my eyebrows for me, cursing me for what she calls my 'crushingly natural arch.'

One night, Alice is putting delicate finger curls in my hair when she starts to talk about how her mother had the most beautiful mane, like sealskin. Mae Steele née Gamble was dismissed from her place of employment when it was discovered she was eight months pregnant with Alice – a fact she had concealed through increasingly painful physical measures for nearly six months. She'd been a chambermaid for a rich Los Angeles family – 'not the Chandlers, but close.'

Mae confided in her daughter Alice the

toil of the job, and the many indignities. Especially, the monthly job of dyeing the woman of the house's pubic hair. 'Once, she asked me if I'd ever done it to myself,' Alice's mother told her daughter. 'I said no, but that I once shaved mine in the shape of a heart for a man. Her jaw dropped to her knees. For about three seconds. And then she decided she liked the idea and she asked me to help her do it. It wasn't for her husband, of course. The Jap gardener. Who was a big favorite in the neighborhood, let me tell you.

'Of course, the man who asked me to shave mine was her husband. When he finally saw what she had done, weeks later, he was furious. Because he knew. He knew that I had something over him, that she and I were that close.'

These sidelong revelations, conveyed so casually, and then an hour later we are seated in sparkling, red-hued nightclubs in Hollywood, nights with cigarette after cigarette, cracked crab on silver plates, and maybe one too many Seven & Sevens.

Three hours later still, my head slung down, chest ringing, I can't stop the quaking fun house feel, bright pops and tingling sparkles, hand clutching, fist twisting in my belly.

Suddenly, Alice's enormous black eyes are

looming beside me.

'Hold on there, darling,' warm and then pealing into a laugh. 'Haven't you ever been tight before?'

Not like this, I try to say, but the thought of speaking seems unimaginable, Alice's hand on my neck, in my hair, trying to hold me up like a ventriloquist's dummy.

'–get you home safe and sound before one of these pretty boys can get his hands on you when my back is turned. Bill will wonder where we–'

And driving home and lights passing over me and I sit in the passenger seat trying to listen, trying to listen to Alice's rustling voice. She is telling me how she saw her mother on television the night before, her long dead mother, and had nightmares all night. It was an old musical and she couldn't remember the name, never remembered the names. As Alice watched the movie, her mother's face suddenly popped out of a row of dancing girls in satin bathing suits. 'Like some horrible jack-in-the-box.' She laughs, her voice rising, quavering uncomfortably.

'This was in the early thirties, before she hung it all up. She couldn't keep up with her union dues, and there were other problems, too.' Alice's voice jingles in my ears, and I try to concentrate, try to hold on to her words, the secrets she may be revealing.

'She moved us out to Hermosa Beach and laid low for several months before getting her maid job. Hard times, and no one suffered more than that woman. At everyone's hands, but especially her own.'

She pauses, looks out the window into the hills, eyes heavy with dread. Then adds, 'If she'd had more of a taste for pleasure, like her husband, she'd have been better off.'

Then adds, 'Did you know. She committed suicide by eating ant paste.'

Then, 'Don't take this the wrong way,' she confides with a ghost of a smile, leaning over as we pull into the driveway, mouth nearly to my ear, 'but it wasn't soon enough.'

For two months, we all fall into an easy schedule. Alice and I carpooling to school. Thursday night dinners. Sundays spent at my brother's, ending with a big Sunday dinner. Sometimes, bowling on Fridays. A double date. The main difference is I spend more time with Alice and almost never see Bill alone for more than a few minutes. It is jarring at first, but I know that it is only natural. They are newlyweds. And Alice is working so hard to make a home.

During the school day, if I have a free period, I sometimes walk by Alice's classroom, just to see. Occasionally, I notice a faraway look in her eyes as she teaches. She is very present, talking seamlessly, directing everything. But her eyes are slick, silver things not connecting to anything, just hanging there, unfixed. And sometimes her body starts to look that way, too. Not tight and taut and jumping like usual, but loose, with slow and elongated movements, punctuated by hands touching everything lightly, running along the sewing machines, sliding along the windowsill, passing over the girls' shoulders, touching everything, but only faintly, fleetingly, like a ghost.

It reminds me of my days volunteering at the county hospital, and the way some patients would always touch you, and the touch was warm and slippery and the morphine tanks dripped endlessly, endlessly.

'Don't you ever get tired of it?' Alice is smoking and driving with equal intensity. It is a bright Monday morning.

'Of what?'

'Of having to be at school. Of having to be in front of them, of having them come up to your desk, in the hallways, in the cafeteria. Always wanting to talk to you. And then, the other teachers, always talking about their classes, about lesson plans, about the students, about the principal, about faculty meetings and curriculum. All the time. All day long.'

I wave her smoke out of my face and say, 'Well, it's the nature of the job. Everyone takes these jobs, chooses teaching because they *do* care, right?'

She looks at me, blowing smoke from her lower lip and smiling faintly. 'I notice you didn't say "we."'

'What do you mean?'

'You didn't say, "*We* take these jobs because *we* care."'

'I was speaking generally,' I say.

She doesn't say anything, her eyes darting at the traffic. I can't tell if she is thinking of a response, or if she's already moved on.

'I've always known I was going to be a teacher,' I add.

She nods vaguely, hitting her horn lightly as a car threatens to force its way into her lane.

'You'll get used to it,' I say.

'You'll come to enjoy it,' I continue. 'Truly. You'll come around.'

I can't stop talking. Somehow, it's me now who can't stop.

The sense always that there is a ticking time bomb ... and then, quite suddenly, it seems to be ticking faster.

It is a month or so before final exams, and I'm in the main office, where the attendance secretary is helping me track down an errant student.

'Don't take it personally, Miss King.' She clucks her tongue. 'Peggy's been missing all of her classes. We're going to have to call her mother.'

'All right,' I say. As I turn, I collide with Principal Evans, his vested chest nearly knocking me down.

'I thought I heard you, Miss King,' he says. 'Come into my office for a moment, will you?'

He opens the door for me with his usual formality.

'Have a seat. I have a small favor to ask.'

'Yes, sir.'

'When we hired your sister–'

'Sister-in-law.'

'Sister-in-law. When we hired her last fall it was under the precondition – the state-dictated precondition – that we would receive a copy of her certification from ... what was it...' He began thumbing through

61

the file in front of him.

'Van Nuys Community College,' he reads aloud, then looks up at me, over his reading glasses.

'Right.'

'Well, somehow we never received the paperwork from Van Nuys. Or from Lomita, where she taught for ... a semester.'

'Really.' I want to be more surprised than I am.

'I'm sure it's merely an oversight.' He smiles serenely.

'I'm sure. Why – may I ask, why are you asking me and not Mrs. King herself?'

'Well, you see, I didn't want her to feel we doubt her,' he says. 'She's very sensitive, you know. A fairly green teacher.'

'I see. I'll be sure to bring it up with her.'

'And I'd hoped to take care of it today, because I have a lunch meeting Wednesday with the superintendent about next year's renewals. Do you know, will she be back tomorrow?'

'Pardon me?'

'Well, I might have broached the subject with Mrs. King herself, delicately, but her illness–'

'Illness?' Alice had seemed fine when we drove to school that morning.

'Oh, I assumed you generally drove in together. She's out sick today. Apparently some sort of flu.'

'Right,' I say, rising. 'I'll speak with her tonight.'

'Righto.'

As I walk out, head suddenly throbbing, I try to guess at what point Alice might have slipped out of school. At what point she gave up her pretense of coming to work and drove away. Perhaps she felt ill once she arrived.

'Miss Harris, have you seen Mrs. King today?'

'No, no,' she says, thumbing through her card file. 'She called in sick.' She waves a card in front of me. 'She phoned when I first arrived, seven A.M.'

'Thank you,' I say.

That night, I call my brother to tell him about the missing paperwork. I speak to him in simple, even tones, trying to keep my voice free from any concern or doubt or judgment.

Like the detective he is, he asks a series of questions I am in no position to answer, questions about how the school or the college must have bungled the process, why he and Alice hadn't been told sooner. Then, he assures me that he will take care of it.

'There must have been some mistake, some kind of filing error or something,' he says, and even over the phone I can somehow see his brow wrinkled in a gesture so old it seems timeless.

'Don't worry,' he says, for the third time.

'I'm not worried, Bill.'

'I'll drive to Van Nuys myself if necessary,' he adds.

'Fine. How was work–'

'–Gee, I wish they'd called me sooner. Evans, I mean. I hate for him to think... I want everything to go smoothly.'

'Is Alice there now?' I ask, as casually as I can manage.

'No, she's out. She's got some meeting. A neighborhood thing, I guess. Couldn't be school-related, or you'd be there, too, right?' he says, and I'm not sure if it is a question or not.

'Right,' I say, deciding, in an instant, not to bring up that Alice had left school before it began. I don't know why I don't tell him. Something in his voice. Instead, the revelation hovers in my throat, too momentous to spill forward. I say nothing.

Then, not a week later, the next head-jerking puzzle.

I am walking into the home ec lab to meet up with Alice for our carpool home. The cavernous room, with its half dozen kitchen units for students to practice making beef bourguignon, is dark, lit only by faint late-afternoon sun. Past the kitchenettes and through the set of sewing machines, I can see Alice standing in front of her desk, my view partially obstructed by sewing dummies.

I pause for a second, because I think I hear her speaking to someone and I wonder if it is a student she might be reprimanding, or counseling, and I don't want to interrupt.

Quickly, however, I can see she is distraught in a way she wouldn't be with a student. The low murmuring becomes more fervent. I step slightly to my side and see the profile of a man leaning against the edge of her desk, facing her. The dark furrow of his brows juts out, and as I inch closer, I can see the edges of a steel blue sharkskin suit.

'Well, how would I know she wasn't going to go through with it? I only know what she told me.'

Then, the deep, indecipherable tones of the man. Then, her again:

'Did she give you the rest? I told her not to do it. I knew it would turn out this way.'

She raises the back of her hand to her forehead. I twist around one of the kitchen counters and see him. He doesn't move at all as they speak, but she moves constantly, winds her arms around herself, scuffing her heels on the floor anxiously.

'She's digging her own grave as far as I'm concerned. That's his story, anyway. I can't promise anything, but she knows better. Christ.'

Her head bobs wildly. I still can't hear him, even as I pass the kitchen units and near the sewing machines, about twenty feet from them. He never moves at all, so still, issuing the low tones of confidence and placidity.

'Christ, why do you think she ... damn it, anyway. Well, she's made her bed and now...'

Alice's foot taps staccato, and suddenly she looks up from her own frantic tapping to the man. He meets her gaze, and then, as if feeling my struck gaze upon him, looks over to me.

'Hello there,' he says calmly, pausing a cool, languorous moment before moving out of his leaning slouch and standing upright. The eyes are the thing – like a Chinaman's. The heaviest lids you ever saw, barely any pupil can squeak through. Cushiony lids and puffy lower rims un-balanced by angular black brows.

Alice's head turns suddenly, jarringly to me, her eyes wide and glassy. Then she quickly smiles and runs over.

'Oh, honey, Lora,' she coos sweetly, and with surprising sincerity. 'Let me introduce you.' She hurries over to me, grabs my hands in her frosty ones, and tugs me back with her.

The man, hat in one hand, holds out his other toward me. 'Good to meet you, Miss King. I've heard...' He trails off, touching his mouth to my hand, fingertips touching the back of my wrist so fleetingly I wonder if I imagine it.

'This is an old friend,' Alice says, tugging at the sleeves of her dress and standing very straight.

'Oh?' I say politely, taking my hand back and burying it safely in my dress pocket.

'I know Alice from when she was a little girl with curlicues and pantaloons.' He winks at me, eyes, face impenetrable, voice soft and low. Utterly unreadable. Is he teasing? Is he lying? Is he sharing a sweet truth?

'Family friends?' I find myself asking, when no one says anything.

'You could say. Seems we've always known each other.' A soft pause and a long arm out to Alice's shoulder as Alice smiles indecipherably. 'But I've been living in Mexico for a while.'

'But you're back now.' Alice looks up at him. 'Isn't it wonderful that you're back? Make new friends but keep the old, as they say.'

Alice wrings her hands and rubs at her watch, pretending not to look at the time, and then abruptly, broadly, she does look, as if in a stage gesture.

'Oh, Lora, it's late, isn't it?'

67

'Yes,' I say. 'Should we go?'

Alice nods anxiously and grabs her purse and gloves from the desk, navigating her way behind him.

'I never did get your name,' I find myself asking.

'Joe Avalon,' he says serenely, putting on his French gray felt hat. 'Miss King, the pleasure has been mine.'

In the car afterward, Alice chatters away about her troublesome fifth-period class, about Nancy Turner, who is going to perform a monologue at the state drama competition, about the Handler girl with the dirty neck whose mother seems to have left town with a marine. She unleashes a stream of talk the likes of which I haven't heard since the night I first met her. A long rant filled with comments, thoughts, and questions for which she leaves no room for answers. Finally, 'Isn't he the nicest fellow? He's an old family friend and he's always helped me out of jams. He just always seems to turn up when I'm in trouble, and for that, I'll always be grateful to him.'

'So you're in trouble now?' I ask, turning the steering wheel as we enter their drive.

'No, no, of course not. I didn't mean *now*. Just in the past, things I owe him for. Not that he expects more than a thanks. But I say it all just to suggest what a fine fellow he is. My friend Maureen, who dated him for a while, used to say, 'a stand-up guy.' That's what he is. Though I'm sure you couldn't tell that from the quick exchange, but even though he looks a little ... *you know*, he's really the *kindest* man you'll ever meet. I should have him over for dinner some night now that he's back in town. I'd really like Bill to meet him. They'd get along like a house on fire, I *know*. Don't you think? Well, maybe not. Oh, here we are.'

And I remember this: a slow, slow turn of her head from me to the house. I remember it occurring in actual slow motion, dragged out, and her head turned and her lit, blazing eyes transforming instantly into coal weights, her face a slow, pale blur studded with heavy, inkblot eyes turning to the house, turning and turning off like a windup toy shutting down and shut ... ting ... off.

That night in my apartment, and other nights, too, burrowed under the covers, I watch the shadows on the wall and think of meeting men, meeting men like in movies, and meeting men like Alice and her mysterious friends seem to – seem to at least in Alice's stories – men met on buses between stops, in the frozen foods aisle, at Woolworth's when buying a spool of thread, at the newsstand, perusing *Look*, in hotel lobbies, at supper clubs, while hailing cabs or looking in shop windows. Men with smooth felt hats and pencil mustaches, men with Arrow shirts and shiny hair, men eager to rush ahead for the doors and to steady your arm as you step over a wet patch on the road, men with umbrellas just when you need them, men who hold you up with a firm grip as the bus lurches before you can reach a seat, men with flickering eyes who seem to know just which coat you are trying to reach off the rack in the coffee shop, men with smooth cheeks smelling of tangy lime aftershave who would order you a gin and soda before you even knew you wanted one.

These men weren't like the men with whom I went to the pictures: Archie Temple, the chemistry teacher, who never got further than rubbing his rough lips half-heartedly against mine, or Fred Cantor, the insurance salesman who sold Bill his policy and took me to Little Bavaria once a month or so for long, cocktail-drenched dinners. While I seldom got past the first, small glass of sweet wine, Fred could go for hours, jollily imbibing and telling stories of his combat duty in the Pacific. Not always but often there would be an awkward, searching embrace in the front seat of Fred's burgundy Buick. A few beery kisses and Fred would get ideas, and before I knew it, he was pressing my hair against the side door window as I tried to peel away from him.

Where were the golden boys of my high school days, the boys with sweet breath and shy smiles, with proud gaits and long lashes, the boys who sat with you for hours in the booth at the local five-and-dime just hoping for a promise, a promise to go to a dance or listen to records with you at Dutton's Hi Fi or to share a paper plate at the church social?

Though I knew these boys, held their sweet, damp hands in mine only a handful of years ago, they were now like sketches in a yellowed paperback, a photo album from many generations past. When we moved to Los Angeles to live near our godparents, we were only sixteen and nineteen. What we left behind remained a half-imagined reverie of half-opened adolescence, caught now forever between curiosity and harsh awakening.

The thing about Lois...

Alice's friend Lois Slattery has a kind of crooked face, one perpetually bloodshot eye just higher than the other, and that Pan-Cake makeup you often see on what Alice calls 'girls on the make.' She begins periodically appearing at Bill and Alice's, each time without warning. Somehow, I end up, over and over again, having conversations with her. Each time thinking, Poor Lois, in a few years, she'll have a slattern look to match her name.

Her clothes are sometimes very expensive but never look like her own, are either too big or too small, or are well-cut and well-made but someone has stepped on the hem, or the collar has a cigarette burn on it. These flaws aren't, as I first thought, because Lois can only afford secondhand clothing. In fact, the garments are often new, bought that day and already with splatters on the lace edging, or the heel loose. It is as simple as this: she has a complicated life and her clothes can't help but show it. It is all part of her unique disheveled glamour.

As it turns out, Lois is less an actress than a professional extra and a sometime dancer. She takes acting classes in West Hollywood. But most of all she seems to go out dancing and drinking with girlfriends or enlisted men or publicity men.

She is the kind of woman whose face you try to commit to memory because you feel something might happen to her at any minute and you'll have to remember that left dimple, the burn mark from a curling iron on her temple, the beauty mark next to her eye, the small tear in her earlobe, from an earring tugged too far.

'I hooked up with this fella lived in Hancock Park,' Lois says out of the corner of her mouth, cigarette dancing lazily. 'Had a gold telephone, that was how high-hat he was.'

I've never heard a real person talk like this. 'How long did you date?'

'We never dated,' she says matter-of-factly, unstrapping her high heels as ashes fly from her hanging cigarette. 'But he was a swell guy. He used to take me dancing and to fine parties up in the Hills, and then, very late, we'd drive over to Musso's for an omelet and one last martini. He once introduced me to Harry Cohn, the big studio guy. Oh my, was he a real blowhard. But it ended badly. With this fella, I mean.'

'What happened?'

'Let's just say'– she flings her shoes onto the floor and props her feet up on the coffee table– 'he had some bad habits.'

'Other women?'

'Even more pressing interests, honey. I'm an open-minded gal, God knows, but even I got my limits.'

'Do you ever run into him?'

'Nah. He moved to Mexico last I heard. I was looking for him to get back some of my clothes and a brand-new straw hat when I ran into Joe Avalon. He was staking out his place looking to collect on some debts owed. It got pretty complicated.'

'I didn't know you knew him, too.' Hearing her say his name gives me a start.

Lois punches out her cigarette and begins to apply a bright lipstick without a mirror. 'Everybody knows Joe, honeybunch. *Everybody.*'

'Did Alice introduce you?'

'Oh, gosh, peach, it don't work like that.'

'What do you mean?'

She places her palms together and twists her wrists in opposite directions in a gesture that seems as though it is supposed to mean something to me.

'Time, Lora, works different in your world.' She twists her wrists back again.

'To me, I've always known Joe Avalon. He was the number-one cherry picker on my block. He changed all our diapers, tweaked our mamas' teats. He was the glimmer in my papa's eye. He lived on the rooftop of every house on our block, and could slither down the chimney at night. He was, is, and always will be your four-leaf clover and dangerous as hell. He's always been here. This town will always have guys like him, as long as it keeps going.'

This is the longest speech Lois has ever given me. I won't forget it.

As we hurtle toward the end of the school year, I see less of Alice on the weekends. Her teaching and her swelling social schedule fill every minute. Still, she seems unable to stop. It is around this time that she begins suffering from what she calls her 'old affliction,' migraine headaches, hissing pain so severe she feels her own skull will crush her. These headaches send her into dark rooms with cool, oscillating fans for hours, even days on end. 'It's related to my cycles,' she confides nonchalantly. 'So there's nothing I can do about it.'

The headaches are almost daily occurrences by the time Bill's baseball league starts up its season. She makes most of the games, putting on a brave face, but I fill in when the pain becomes too much. It helps make Bill less worried. He never wants to leave Alice alone, but she insists, setting a cramped hand on his chest and swatting him away.

Long hours in the bleachers, hands wrapped in knitting or spread out over *McCall's,* the investigators' wives sit, and often I sit with them. Tonight, it is with the blond and blunt-nosed Edie Beauvais.

'Lora, I'm *desperate*. I've got to get pregnant. We've been waiting for so long now.'

She runs her tiny hand up and down her arm, which is flecked with goose bumps from the chilling night air. 'We had this fantasy of getting pregnant on our wedding night. That's what I expected. But now... I just want it so bad, Lora.'

Edie is the young wife of Charlie Beauvais, one of Bill's coworkers at the investigators' office. Although he was always willing to take a coworker who'd had a hard day out for a beer, and he'd always stop in at the local tavern when an after-work gathering was under way, Bill never had many friends. Besides, most of the men in his department are either heavy drinkers or gamblers or both, or are wrapped up in the politics of the office. But Charlie has been a kind of mentor to Bill, showing him the ropes when the other men resented Bill's quick rise, which they attributed to luck or imagined connections.

'But you're so young, Edie,' I say, watching the action absentmindedly, watching Charlie waving his hat, waving a player in, laughing mightily, big white teeth against his stubble-creased face. 'You've got plenty of time.'

'I know,' she says. 'I've got nothing but time.' She stifles a long sigh by dipping her chin and tucking her mouth into her collarbone.

Edie is twenty-three, Charlie's second wife. Born in Bakersfield, she was straight out of modeling school when they met four years before. She had talked her way out of a speeding ticket, claiming a 'feminine emergency.'

'Are you going to help out at the fundraiser again?' I ask.

'Sure, sure,' she says, eyelashes fluttering, trying gamely to focus on the action. 'Where's Alice?'

'She wasn't feeling well,' I say.

Edie nods vaguely, watching Charlie bounding in from the infield, removing his hat and rubbing his crew cut vigorously.

'Looking good, honeybunch,' she coos, waving and twisting in her seat. Charlie's face bursts out into a grin. It seems to explode over his whole rubbery face as he turns to join his teammates on the bench.

'When are you going to get yourself one of those? A husband, I mean,' Edie asks as we watch Bill take a few practice swings.

'So you think I'm in danger of old maid status too?'

She turns to me with a smile. 'Don't you want to have a house and kids and nice things?'

I look at her with her blond lashes, eyebrows penciled with delicacy, face so fresh and flat and empty, as only California faces can be. 'It's hard to find a man like Charlie, though, isn't it?'

'Hmmm,' Edie says, eyes roaming dreamily back to the game, to the shoving match that seems about to unfold between Bix Carr and Tom Moran, who always fought, over sports, old debts, patrol assignments, cars.

I am supposed to say these things, the things I should want. It is what you say. I look at Edie, looking at the other tired, careless faces on the bleachers, hair tucked in curlers under scarves, bodies straining or flaccid, pregnant or waiting to be.

We watch as Bill and Charlie separate the men, and Bill talks them down, his hand on Bix's shoulder, Bix nodding, cooling. Tom abashed, kicking the dirt.

'I'm going home, sugar.' Edie sighs, stumbling forlornly down the bleachers.

I wave good-bye.

An hour later, the game finally over, Bill wanders over. 'Where's Edie? Charlie's looking for her.'

'She left,' I say.

'Oh. Really? That's funny. Charlie–'

Tom Moran comes running up behind Bill, slapping him mightily on the back. 'Billy, where's that gorgeous wife tonight?'

Bill extends a hand to help me descend the bleachers. 'Under the weather.'

'Too bad. Don't mind gazing up at her.'

Bill looks over at him for a second, as if caught between annoyance and good humor.

'You know.' Tom shrugs, grinning at me anxiously. 'She's different than the others. Than the other wives. Ain't she?'

I smile faintly, and Bill tilts his head, unsure how to respond.

I know this isn't the first time he's heard these comments. I've seen the way they look at her. They watch her when she comes to City Hall, they watch her at the social events, they watch the way she walks, hips rolling with no suggestion of provocation but with every sense that she knows more than any of the rest. A woman like that, they seem to be thinking, a woman like that has lived.

Their wives come from Orange County, they come from Minnesota or Dallas or St. Louis. They come from places with families, with sagging mothers and fathers with dead eyes and heavy-hanging brows. They carry their own promise of future slackness and clipped lips and demands. They have sisters, sisters with more babies, babies with sweet saliva hanging and more appliances and with husbands with better salaries and two cars and club membership. They iron in housedresses in front of the television set or by the radio, steam rising, matting their faces, as the children with the damp necks cling to them, sticky-handed. They are this. And Alice ... and Alice...

Charlie Beauvais, he once said it. Said it to

Bill in my earshot. He said, Don't worry, pal, don't worry. It's not that they want her. It's just they have this feeling – and they're off, Billy, they're way off – but they have this sense that, somehow behind that knockout face of hers, she's more like the women they see on the job, on patrol, on a case, in the precinct house. Women with stories as long as their rap sheets, as their dangling legs...

Struggling to sleep in the guest bedroom after helping clean up the damage from a late party, I can hear Bill and Alice talking on the back porch, talking soft and close.

'How is it that Lora hasn't been snatched up, anyhow?'

'What?'

'You know. I'm just surprised she isn't married. I mean, you could say the same about me, until I met you. It's just that she seems the type to be married.'

'She *is* the type to be married. She'll get married.'

'I'm sure. I just wondered why she hasn't yet, darling. Just curious. She's so sweet and such a warm girl, and–'

'She was almost married once. About three years ago.'

I am listening as if it isn't me somehow

they are speaking about, as if it were someone else entirely. I hold my breath and pretend to sink into the very walls.

'Oh? Did you scare him off, big brother?'

'It wasn't like that. He was a good friend of mine. A guy who used to be on the force when I first started.'

'Did you play matchmaker?'

'Sort of. It just kind of happened naturally. We'd all spend time together, go to movies. He was a good guy, and it made sense.'

His tone is shifting, from cautious to grave, and she begins to respond accordingly.

'So what happened?'

'They began getting serious just as he had to leave the force. TB. It was rough, but she stood by him. You know, that's how she is.'

'Oh, dear. Did he–'

'No, no. He eventually had to go to a sanatorium, way up by Sacramento or something. He didn't want her to wait for him. He was a shell of the guy he'd once been. Down to a hundred and twenty pounds. He couldn't bring himself to continue with her. He did the right thing. He said, "Bill, I can't let her tie herself to me like a sash weight," he said. So he broke it off.'

'He isn't still up there–'

'No. They wrote to each other for a while, but it wasn't the same. Last I heard, he married one of the nurses there and they settled. He works for an insurance company or something.'

It really wasn't like this, was it? Was that how simple it was, so explicable in a few sentences, a few turns of phrase? Wasn't it months of high drama, so wrenching, so unbearably romantic that I'd conveniently forgotten that I never really cared that deeply for the amiable, square-jawed Hugh Fowler to begin with?

It had absorbed all the emotional energies of Bill and myself for a fall and winter and an early spring, and then, suddenly, it was as though he'd never been a part of our lives at all. His second month at River Run Rest Lodge and we couldn't remember when we'd next be able to make the long drive up the coast.

And then other things emerged, other things that left no room, no time, no space for that sweet-faced young man who, so ill, would shudder against me despite his height, his gun holster, his still-broad (but not for long) shoulders. Was that it?

'How very tragic,' says Alice. 'Like out of a movie. It could be a movie. Poor Lora.'

'She'll find someone and it'll be right,' Bill says firmly. I feel my eye twitch against the pillow. I press my hand to it, hard.

'Well, I'm going to help.'

'Oh, Alice, I wouldn't–'

'I know lots of wonderful men. Men from the studios.'

'I don't think Lora would want to date anyone in the movie business. That's not Lora.'

'Oh, brothers don't know,' Alice says. 'And I can't bear to see her with these sad sacks from school. These men with the saggy collars and shoes like potatoes. I'm going to get her with a real sharpshooter. If you had your way...'

'Alice, you don't know Lora. She won't–'

'Just watch me.'

I can hear her smile even if I don't see it. It doesn't seem real, that this is me they are talking about. I look out the window, at the heavy jacaranda branches trembling gently against the pane. I think, for a moment, about the men Alice seems to know and it's hard to believe they really exist. That they could enter my life, my small world. What would it mean if they came crashing in the same way Alice has?

As my cheek leans against the glass, I realize suddenly how hot my face is. I press my hand to it, surprised.

It is a long time before I fall asleep.

With this forewarning, I am prepared when, after one of what Alice refers to as my 'sad sack' dates, she phones me and announces she is ready to play matchmaker.

'His name is Mike Standish. Can you believe it? I call him Stand Mannish.'

'What does he do? He's not an actor.'

'No, no, of course not. He's with the publicity department. He's delicious, Lora. He's a huge, strapping man. He's like a tree, a redwood. He's a lumberjack.'

I am always surprised by what Alice thinks might make a man sound attractive to me.

'I don't know.'

'Lora, he's very smart and accomplished. For God's sake, he went to Col-*um*-bia University.'

'He doesn't want to date a schoolteacher in Pasadena.'

'He wants to date *you*. I set it all up. He's taking you to Perino's and then to the Cocoanut Grove. The only question is what you should wear.'

'When is all this supposed to happen?'

Why not, for God's sake. Why not.

'One thing, Lora, one thing,' she says, and it's almost a whisper, a voice burrowing straight into my head. 'This is what he does: first thing, he warns you that he's going to charm you, and that warning becomes part of his charm.'

'Hey, Shanghai Lil, come over here,' my brother says, waving his arm toward Alice.

'I think that you no love me still.' She pouts, imitation geisha, as she pads over in her brand-new Anna May Wong – style silk pajamas.

'See how nice it can be staying home on a Saturday night.' He smiles peacefully, tucking her into his arms.

'Until you get the call.' She sighs.

'Not tonight. Promise.'

'Your sister will have fun enough for us all.' She turns from inside the serge curl of my brother's arm and looks to me.

'Oh? Where are you going?' He straightens up suddenly and peeks out over Alice's blue silk to see me.

I pause.

'Just to dinner, I think. And then dancing maybe.' I stare at my lipstick, then dab a bit more on for good measure.

'Mike Standish shows a lady a good time.' Alice slides out from Bill's arms and slinks over to me.

'We can go out, too, Alice. I just thought–'

'That's not what I meant,' Alice says, curling up in front of me as I sit in the wing chair.

'Maybe we can join them. I–'

'No, no, no, darling.' She reaches out for my lipstick to add still more. Her face looms over me, and her eyes hang big as saucers. 'Besides, they don't want old marrieds along, believe me.'

'I'm sure we'd be glad for the company,' I say, blotting with the handkerchief she holds out to me. 'The more the merrier.' 'I'd like to meet this Standish guy,' my brother says suddenly. 'Have him in for a drink.'

Alice shakes her head and slides back into his lap. 'Easy, Judge Hardy. You're not her father, after all. You'll meet him soon enough. Besides, doesn't Lora want *some* privacy? Some life separate from family?'

She looks at me as she says it, and there is a wistfulness there, a kind wistfulness that, despite everything, I find myself warming to, and secretly thanking her for.

Two hours later, this:

'I could tell you stories, honey.' Mike Standish smiles. 'Stories to make Fatty Arbuckle blush. The four-o'clock-in-the-morning calls I've gotten, the places I've had to peel them off of the floor, the circus freaks I've had to pay off to keep these little indiscretions, these quaint peccadilloes out of the papers.'

'You sound proud of yourself.'

'As they say, life is too short to bother with

Puritan hypocrisies. Besides, it's not me racking up time in the booth with Father McConnell. I just clean up,' he says, still smiling, rubbing his hands together as if to wash them.

'My grandmother would have called those devil's dues,' I say noncommittally, removing the maraschino from the bottom of my drink.

'Your grandmother didn't know what she was missing.' He winks, cuff links flashing in the soft light, summoning the waiter over for another round.

A few days later, as I arrive to help Alice make cookies for the senior banquet, I see that Lois Slattery is back again. I take a chair as Alice fusses over the moon and star shapes. The cookie cutter, in her frustration, keeps slipping from her hand.

'Lois, if you get one cigarette ash near these cookies, I'm going to tear your hair out.'

'Better men than you have tried,' Lois slurs, unaccountably nodding to me before leaning back in her chair.

'I just don't have the patience today.' Alice sighs, wiping her face with the back of her hand.

'Can't the blue bird scouts or whoever manage with store-bought?'

'No, no.' Alice's crimson-tipped fingers

steady themselves and she manages to get the first perfectly cut star safely onto the sheet.

Lois turns and looks at me. 'She gave up Tinseltown for this.'

'What a sacrifice,' Alice says with a faint smile. 'I saw enough of the business from my mother to know where it gets you. I didn't even want to end up working for the studios, but who would turn down union wages?'

I nod, as she seems to want affirmation.

'Still,' she adds, 'it was a rotten job, running measuring tape over starlets all day.'

'That was how we met,' Lois says, eyeing me.

Alice, intently at work, raises her hand to Lois to ensure silence as she lifts a pair of moonbeam cookies onto the sheet.

Lois bends forward again with a deep red smile. 'You know what that looks like?'

Alice looks at Lois expressionlessly but with a firm lock of the eyes.

Lois breaks the gaze and turns to me. 'Do you recognize it, Loreli?'

'I guess that'd be a moonbeam, no?'

'Does it remind you of anything?'

'No,' I say, feeling like the girl at school who was never let in on the game.

'Relating to a certain brother darling?' Lois waves her cigarette over the cookie and then toward the kitchen door. Alice stares motionless.

'Pardon?'

'You *know.* I can't say I've seen it myself, but ... the scar, doll.'

'Oh, the scar from his accident,' I say, trying not to picture the horrible night of the assault. The scar came from the sharp edge of the radiator when he fell after the baseball bat blows from the young suspect. It is right above his hip.

'I haven't seen it since the hospital,' I add. 'I suppose I've never seen it as a scar. Only as a wound.' I feel my throat go a little dry. It seems strange to have us all sitting here, dwelling on this.

'Lois,' Alice says with an edge, hands still, hovering over the cookies. Lois returns the tough gaze, bites her lip a bit, shrugs with effort, and looks down at her pointy, scuffed shoes.

Later that night, at the fabulous Alice-inspired cocktail party at the Beauvais house, Alice and I drink gimlets together, and the heat wilting us, the crowd pounding in, we draw closer and I've forgotten everything but how much, everything else aside, she only wants it all to be good, to be good and fine.

'Lois, I told Lora to – I mean' – Alice giggles, correcting herself tipsily– 'Lora, I told *Lois* to stop coming by.'

'Oh,' I say, helping her steady her tilting drink.

'Bill doesn't really like her around. He thinks she's bad news. Which, of course, she is.'

'She is?'

'Nothing serious, of course,' Alice assures. 'I'm just trying to wean her off me, but it's hard because we've known each other so long.'

Then Alice tugs me closer to her, nearly pressing her mouth to my ear as we nestle on the Beauvaises' sofa. It is then that she tells me how they met, years before, at the studio.

Alice was fitting Lois, a young extra, into an Indian Girl costume, feathered headband, short tunic straight from a gladiator picture, pure Hollywood. When she was adjusting the hem, she saw the abrasions on the insides of Lois's thighs, shallow like slightly large pockmarks.

'So glamorous,' Lois had said, not even looking down at Alice, kneeling beside her, needles in her mouth. 'I didn't know the skirt would be so short.'

'It won't pick up on camera,' Alice had said.

'I thought that once, and the next thing I knew, the camera was moving under my spread legs.'

Alice hadn't said anything but smiled just enough to keep the needle in her mouth as she pinned the hem.

'You can never tell when a camera's going to be between your spread legs,' Lois had continued, seeing Alice's smile.

'You sure can't,' Alice said, dropping the pin too fast. 'Oops! Did you get poked?'

At that, Lois had let out a long, quiet, drawl-like laugh, and Alice had laughed too.

'You have a lot of history,' I say.

Alice sighs and raises her eyebrows. 'That we do.' Then, suddenly, 'I'm sorry about earlier, though. About what Lois said about the scar.'

'What do you mean?'

'I don't want you to think I tell her all kinds of private things about Bill.'

'I don't,' I say, even as, for the first time, I wonder if she does exactly this.

'Truth is, Lora…'

Truth is, Lora…

Don't think I'm trashy…

Truth is, I think his scars are beautiful, Alice whispers, face red.

I think they're beautiful, she repeats. Don't you?

Then comes the first step from which there is no turning back.

As the final bell rings for the day, Alice grabs my arm in the corridor.

'I know we have a staff meeting, but can we miss just this one?'

'You go on. I'll make excuses and get a ride home with Janet,' I say, wondering what arch looks will fly at Alice missing yet another faculty meeting.

'Actually, Lora, I was wondering if you could come with me.'

'Come with you?'

'I have to go see Lois. She's sick and I want to check in on her.'

'That's fine, but why do you need me?'

'Please, Lora? I'm worried. It would be such a relief to have you there.'

I look over at her, fingers clasped tightly over the clipboard in her hand. There is such forceful concern that I can't help but agree. I feel glad that Alice would go to such lengths for her friend, that the intensity with which she approaches being my brother's wife is not the only force surging through her.

It is a long drive that involves threading through a series of shaggy and ominous neighborhoods. Alice talks the entire time, almost as though trying to distract me from the gray-boxed bars and barred-window pawnshops that stud the roadways as we finally land on Rosecourt Boulevard. She sings along to the radio when she isn't talking, mostly about the shopping she needs to do and how late she is going to be for dinner guests but that fortunately she has prepared everything in advance, from the cold potato soup to the slow-cooking roast.

'What a horrible name for a place to live,' I murmur as I notice a thickly painted apartment complex to our right. Its large, red-lettered sign darts out from behind a heavy blur of swaying pepper trees, 'Locust Arms Apartments.'

Alice laughs loudly and suddenly, like a bark. Covering her mouth, she says, 'That's where Lois lives.'

I feel my face redden but say nothing as Alice pulls the car into the small lot. We step out and begin walking toward the courtyard.

Watching Alice three steps ahead of me, gliding serenely past each blistered door while I find myself sneaking only furtive glances, I wonder about the places she's lived. Places even worse than the Bunker Hill rooming house.

The place is run-down, but it isn't that.

It's something else. Something I can't quite name. The paper-thin doors, heavily curtained windows, the faint sound of someone chipping ice, relentlessly, the winding drone of a radio playing music without rises or falls, just a sporadic beat, the vague murmur of a neglected cat. Behind all these doors there is something finishing. Dead ends.

Alice knocks pertly on the door marked 7.

'Lucky seven,' she says to me unreadably.

There is the sound of feet running anxiously, and the door flings open so quickly that Alice and I both jump back with a start.

Lois's white face pokes out of the dark interior with an energy I've never seen in her.

'Get in, get in.' She half-stumbles backward, waving at us furiously.

It is hardly larger than a hotel room: a small seating area with a chair and settee, both covered in thick, lime-colored bark cloth, a tiny kitchenette with a counter and two stools, a sagging bed. My eyes keep shifting from one detail to the next: the chipped, brown-ringed porcelain sink, the upturned liquor bottles in the corner, the two chalky glasses that seem, as far as I can tell, to be stuck to the shelf paper adhered to the counter.

Alice, as if to shake me out of it, grabs my arms and sits me down beside her on the unforgiving couch.

'How are you feeling?' she asks as Lois, wearing an expensive-looking appliquéd kimono, paces before us anxiously.

'How do I look?' She turns to us, sweat streaked on her face and neck, raccoon eyes. I can hear the ice chipping again. And a long, low drip tapping from Lois's bathroom.

She turns to Alice. 'Why did you bring her here?'

I look at Alice embarrassedly.

'You called and said you were running a hundred-and-four-degree fever. I thought she could help.' Alice seems eerily calm, even opening her purse and tapping out a cigarette.

Lois's eyes narrow. 'I know why you brought her.'

Alice lights her cigarette and shakes the match out, tossing it on the coffee table.

Standing on the balls of her bright white feet, Lois waits for a response.

Alice merely smiles and exhales a long curl of smoke.

The silence becomes unbearable, and I venture, 'Alice was worried about you.'

Lois looks at me for a second, then fixes her gaze back on Alice, cool, implacable Alice.

'That's not why she brought you, Sis,' Lois says, as if turning something over in her mind. 'She's just calling a bluff.' She rubs the side of her face with the back of her hand, then adds, 'You think you can leave us alone for a minute?'

Although she doesn't look away from Alice as she speaks, she seems still to be talking to me.

Alice's and Lois's eyes are locked, Lois's are working, Alice's possessed of an unreachable calm.

'Okay,' I say, dreading the thought of waiting in that courtyard. I rise and walk to the flimsy front door, shutting it behind me.

I take a few cautious steps to the old concrete fountain in the courtyard's center, bone dry. I have the vague sense that I'll never approach an understanding of what I've just witnessed. Something between women who've known each other for centuries.

Waiting, I watch a tiny, birdlike woman with one shoe in her hand and none on her feet make her quiet way from the parking lot, through the courtyard and to Number 4. Walking with purpose, her eyes focused on the ground, with the funny gait of the barefooted. She pushes on the door with the hand that holds the shoe, and it pops open like the top of a hatbox.

I rise again and walk in slow circles back toward Number 7.

I lean against the outer wall of the apartment, not intending to – but quickly realizing I can – hear Alice and Lois.

It is only patches, fragments.

'...not afraid to bring her...'

'...bring him next time...'

'...is the end of everything...'

'...watching over me to keep me doing what you...'

'...everything she says. You know what he'd do...'

'...Don't you see? ... the end of everything...'

'...that what you want?'

The words, their whispery, insinuating tones, their voices blending together – I can't tell them apart, they seem the same, one long, slithery tail whipping back and forth. My head shakes with the sounds, the hard urgency, and my growing anxiety at being somehow involved in this, even if by accident, by gesture.

The voice – as it seems only one now –becomes abruptly lower, inaudible, sliding from reach. The more I strain, the more I lose to the ambient sounds of the courtyard, the radio, a creaking chair, the cat, the vague clatter of someone knocking shoes together, a bottle rolling.

Suddenly, the door bursts open and Alice is right in front of me.

'All right, she's fine. Let's go.' Alice grasps my arm lightly and begins marching us both across the courtyard.

Surprised and confused, I turn around to see Lois leaning against the doorframe.

'Bye, Sis,' she murmurs, looking calmer and quite still, voice returning to its usual vague drawl.

Alice moves me forward fast, and I keep looking back at Lois until Alice turns us around the corner and Lois disappears behind the faded yellow hacienda wall.

In the car on the long ride home, Alice assures me everything is fine.

'She needs my attention sometimes and will do a lot to get it. It's hard for her to have me married and with my own commitments and not always able to be there. Once I saw she wasn't sick – not really sick – I knew she only wanted to see me *concerned* about her. It's hard for her since I married. But, truth told' – Alice puffs away on a new cigarette– 'she's just going to have to get used to it.

'Right?' She looks at me, waiting for a response.

'Right.' I nod, without knowing to what I am agreeing. The more she speaks, the more I feel convinced that there is an entirely separate narrative at work here, one to which I might never have access. Nor should I want to.

At the polished bar at the Roosevelt Hotel. Corner booth. Gimlets.

Mike Standish leans back and puts forth a

long, rich smile.

'Everyone knew Alice. Everyone in Publicity especially. Most of the women in Costume were old ladies, pinch-faced old maids or pinch-faced young virgins. But Alice... Hell, maybe they all seemed more pinch-faced because Alice was so ... unpinched.'

He pulls a cigarette from his gleaming case, fat onyx in its center. As he taps it leisurely, his smile grows wider. 'She would be there at all hours, walking toward you, slow and twisty, a ball gown hanging off one arm, sometimes a cigarette tucked in those red lips. Jesus.'

He lights his cigarette and blows a sleek stream upward.

'Of course, she wasn't really my type,' he concedes with a half shrug. 'Too much going on all the time. Made you really nervous. Once you started talking to her, she made you feel like the threads in your suit were slowly unraveling.

'Still, she was awfully fun. We'd take her out, the fellows and I. She'd bring along a few friends. We'd go out drinking, to the Hills or on the water, Laguna Beach. To Ensenada once. Once even to Tijuana. No, twice. That's right. Twice.'

'Did you meet Lois Slattery?'

'Who's that?'

'A friend of Alice's.'

'What's she look like?'

'Dark hair, short.'

'That doesn't really narrow it down. Alice seemed to know a lot of girls.'

'Very young-looking. And with slanty eyes, kind of crooked.'

Mike grins suddenly, his hand curling around his face in sudden recollection.

'Oh, yeah. One eye higher than the other. That B-girl.' He squints one eye and looks up. 'Lois? Are you sure? I thought her name was Lisa – or Linda. She came out with us one night. Slumming in... Jesus, some bar in Rosecourt. Oh, yes. Lois, huh?'

He looks at me suddenly. 'You've met her?'

'Yes.'

'I can't picture that, angel.' He hands me his cigarette. 'Well, what do you know?'

I take a quick drag and hand it back. 'What do you mean, "B-girl"?'

'Oh, what the hell do I know?' he says, shrugging handsomely. 'I even had her name wrong.'

'Didn't you think it was strange that Alice would know a ... someone you'd call a B-girl?'

He looks at me, eyes dancing, revealing nothing. Then, he opens his mouth, pauses, and says, plain as that, 'No.'

Suddenly, it is commencement, and then begins a long, rich summer with no classes to teach and lately so much to occupy evenings. I see Mike Standish once or twice a week, but there are also the parties those in Bill and Alice's neighborhood circle hold, and especially Alice herself. These parties always include me, the married couples eager to invite a young single to play with, to engineer setups for, to pepper with questions, reminisce about being young and unattached, an entire life path still unwritten.

As for me, suddenly the world is so much larger than it had been before.

There are gin-drizzled evenings with a few neighbor couples, some of the other teachers and their spouses, a few of Bill's friends from work, along with their wives, everyone laughing and touching arms and elbows, and the bar cart creaking around the room and no kids yet, or the few there are, safely tucked away in gum-snapping babysitters' arms.

Almost every week there is one, usually on Saturday evening. They are cocktail parties, rarely dinner parties, yet they can stretch long into the dinner hour, sometimes beyond. Once in a while, arguments flare up, typically between couples, at times between Bill's friends from the D.A.'s office.

Sometimes there is intrigue spiraling out, whispered conversations by guests slipping into dens or rec rooms, the far corners of the darkened lawns, out by the hibiscus bushes beside the carport, on beds soft with piles of coats.

At first, I go to these parties with Archie Temple, the geology teacher, or Fred Cantor, the salesman, or some setup, usually an awkward one, given the high energy and heavy drinking of these parties.

But when I start seeing Mike Standish more frequently, he comes along, and then we go out afterward, to Romanoff's or even Ciro's.

At all of these parties, Mike thinks everyone there is a hopeless square, except for Alice. But he likes to watch, seated amused on the sofa, sipping his Scotch and making sly comments to me.

Sometimes, a woman flirts with him and he strings her along, winking to me, flashing his gold cuff links, his sleek watch, his slick and slippery eyes. Later, he makes fun of her Mamie Eisenhower bangs or her twitchy eye or her flat accent or her off-the-rack décolletage. And I laugh and laugh no matter who it is or what kindnesses she's shown me. It doesn't matter. I laugh and laugh anyway and don't care.

Alice sometimes dances with the dashing school drama teacher. They do Latin numbers, Cuban routines. She pulls the edge of her satin skirt to her side, tosses her head back, grins darkly, hotly, and everyone watches in admiration as he twirls her, as they twist and lean and then swing back upright and taut.

Bill claps most loudly of all. He watches her, transfixed, and shakes his head with a smile, and when she finishes he walks over to her, puts an arm around her tiny shoulders, looks down at her and marvels, just marvels. How did it happen, he seems to be wondering, that I married this person?

By the evening's third trip to the bathroom, a face caught in the mirror, a smear of what you were a few hours ago. You totter, you catch a smudgy glimpse, you see an eyelash hanging a bit, lipstick bleeding over the lip line. Heel catches on back hem, hand slips on towel rack, grabbing tightly for shell pink guest towel.

There are more than a few times Mike walks me out of the house and we end up back at his place before we head out for a nightclub or show.

The thing about. Mike is he is always ready to go back out again. He knows just how to rub a cold towel on his face and yours, how to fix you both hot coffee and dry toast, how to make a few calls, shift a few reservations, and you both, not a full hour after arriving at the Hillock Tower Apartments, find yourselves sitting straight-backed and freshly groomed in Mike's buttercup yellow roadster.

During the summer, during every past summer so why not this one, I go to the courthouse and have lunch with Bill a few days a week. If he is very busy, it is a quick lunch cart break, the two of us settling at his desk or in the Plaza Las Fuentes over liverwurst or a hot dog. He leans across his desk, shirtsleeves up and suspenders, and tells me as much as he can about a case he is working on. Three times out of four it seems like he is looking for someone who is likely, he says, long gone.

When he first started, I remember always asking him if it was like-in the movies, with finger men and stool pigeons and rats. He'd always laugh and say it both was and wasn't like that, but he could never really explain. When he spoke about his job, it was usually as if he were just a man shuffling papers and making phone calls and conducting interviews across desks and through doorways. This was the way he chose to talk about it.

These lunches seem more important now

that Bill is married. They are nearly the only times I see him alone.

Soon, however, Alice begins to have lunch with Bill too and there aren't enough lunches to go around, given Bill's schedule, which often means eating lunch on the job, driving around and doing his work, whatever it is that day. So, at first, Alice and I drive out together. This doesn't last too long, however, because it feels like a big production. Alice is always perfectly out-fitted, with a new hat, silk flowers on her lapel, her hair done at the salon that morning. By the time we make it to the courthouse, it is late and we draw so much attention that Bill begins to feel as though it looks too 'fancy.'

So we start visiting on alternate weeks. Sometimes, at the last minute, Bill realizes he is going to be free for a quick tuna sand-wich if I can come down, and sometimes we meet at Gus's, a diner halfway between work and home. This way, we can have our talks without trouble. We don't need to tell Alice.

These times remind me of how things were before, after Bill returned from the war and we moved to Pasadena together. Every-thing had settled beautifully. He was so busy with his police training, and I was so busy with my classes and certification training and teaching. But it worked well because we helped each other, and we knew how to unwind at the end of the long days, listening to *Molle Mystery Theatre*, *This Is Your FBI*, and *Inner Sanctum* on the radio, playing Scrabble, Monopoly, Chinese checkers.

He told me some stories of overseas. He brought back a small stack of photos, and he would explain everything to me, saying, 'This was Tom, he was from Virginia and he had a wife and new baby at home, he wrote letters every day,' and 'This one is of me and Popeye, that's what we called him because of the way his jaw stuck out to the side, he was from the Ozarks and he got shot in the neck by a sniper in Berlin, the first one I knew to get it.'

He also had some souvenirs, which he kept in the top drawer of his sideboy. His army-issue pocketknife, a pewter stein, some medals and stripes, even a small, toylike pistol – a Walther PPK, he informed me, not letting me touch it – that he had been allowed to keep when he disarmed a German officer in a skirmish.

The war had been nearly over by the time Bill made it to Europe. He was one of the last drafted, and most of his time overseas was spent in occupied Germany, supervising the rebuilding. He was shot at more than once, mostly in encounters with hostile civilians or stragglers. But he considered himself very lucky, and the experience was, he always said, fundamental to his decision to enter law enforcement. 'Seeing what I saw, people driven to bad things. It made me want to... I don't know how to put it, exactly. It's just, you realize, most people wouldn't go bad either if ... if the *really* bad people, the real animals could be stopped. You stop them and you can save all the rest, Lora. You really can.'

So rare to hear him speak like this, to speak about himself and what he believed. He curled his fist and lightly punched his thigh with it as he sat beside me and spoke. Where did this come from, my brother feeling things so strongly, knowing things so fervently?

When we were children, a man ran over the bicycle of the little deaf girl next door to us. The man plowed over it, and crushed it to the quick. Nancy, that was her name, was only seven and didn't understand it at all, thought nothing could be so wretched as this. She kept crying, and Bill, who'd seen the whole thing, seen the man take the corner of the road too quickly and swerve onto the shoulder and knock it down with a crunch, became so angry that he didn't know what to do. He kept pacing, kicking the dirt as Nancy cried and my grandmother comforted her. The next day he traded in his bicycle, only two months old, for a small girl's bicycle to replace Nancy's.

When my grandparents and Nancy's, and Nancy herself, crying her big blue eyes out, tried to thank him, he wouldn't even look at them. It embarrassed him. That's how he was.

'I think you like Mike Standish a lot.' Alice smiles, shaking crushed coconut into the bowl.

'Sure.' I smile back, handing her a wooden spoon.

'I think' – she plucks two oranges from the glazed fruit bowl – 'that you're falling for him.'

A hot jolt sails through me.

'Don't be silly, Alice.' I help her remove the pith, slicing the membrane from its glaring rind with a knife. 'We're just friends. We enjoy each other's company.'

She begins peeling the pineapple, her fingers heedlessly diving into the spikes. 'It's something else. There's something there,' she says, her hands now sticky with the juice, and my own stinging with the orange flesh. 'Something you like.'

Something about how you are with him.

She splashes some liqueur into the bowl. It drizzles over the sugar crystals, swirled in with the vanilla extract. Our hands are matted with pulp, with juice, with the soft skin of coconut beneath our fingernails. I turn my hand around and lick the heel, feeling the sweet sting. *Why not?*

Mike working a room, patting men on the back, running his softly used hands on the backs of women's necks. It is clear he will go further, rise higher than some of the other men in the publicity department because he never seems too eager. And because he never has the look of a man with something to sell. He is always on the make, but only in the most general, most genial way, a way that suggests he is enjoying the ride while it lasts and shouldn't we all, too?

He can play tennis with the actors, go hunting with the directors, golf with the producers, make the nightclub scene with the new talent. He is always willing to put an ingenue on his arm for the premiere, or walk in with the mistress while the big shot walks with his wife.

He can tell bawdy jokes and read racing forms. He knows the right restaurants to be at and the right times to be at them, he knows the drinks to order, the maître d's to grease. He can tell the studio folk the best place to vacation; he has the steamer trunk company number on hand, the dealer to go to for the latest cars, the company from which to rent the yacht, the tailor to get just the right cut. He knows which lawyers to call and when, which reporters to leak to and which to throw off the scent. These are valuable things for a thirty-two-year-old climber to know. And it always helps that he is from Connecticut and went to Columbia (and nearly graduated) and has the sheen of class and breeding everyone he works for lacks.

There is something very easy about Mike, about being with Mike, about Mike's whole existence. He never has a wrinkle on his suit. His hair is cut once a week, though one never need know how it happens, or where or when, because it occurs in the margins between when I see him and when I see him next. I never see a restaurant check, or worry about hailing a cab, or imagine how it happens that Mike pays his bills or his rent, or his cleaning lady. All the practicalities of his life seem to go on invisibly, effortlessly.

How does he come to own the clothes he wears so immaculately – when does he shop? When does it happen that orange juice and Coca-Cola end up in his refrigerator or the plate of perfectly arranged Kentucky pralines on his kitchen table or the Seagram's and soda water on his bar cart? Even if his cleaning lady purchases these things, or the stores deliver them on a regular order, when does Mike place the order or sit and think about what he wants?

110

When does he deal with the mail on the table? I've seen him run through it, eyes darting at the return address names, and then toss it back down. When does it all happen? Where is all the offscreen time?

It is barely possible to imagine Mike taking a shower. Isn't he always perfectly groomed, crisply cologne-scented, freshly shaved and ready to go? What a disappointment it would be to become truly intimate with him, to stay over past the deliciously mechanical grope on the bed after the long string of martinis and have to see the behind-the-scenes efforts that produce such a clean and cool container of a man.

Exactly when – in what order – these things happened, the *structure*, is hazy, muddled. The moments pop forward, spring out suddenly, and there I am, sometime early that summer, coming by to visit with Bill, maybe go for a drive together. Instead, I find Lois, whom I haven't seen since that day five weeks before at the Locust Arms. She is making herself at home in the bedroom, wearing a lavender feather boa, parts of which are stuck to her face. It looks as though she's been wearing it for days, some of it still fluffy and sleek, like an excited bird, other parts knotted and fraying.

'Lois, each time I see you...'

Lois, each time I see you, I think I've discovered the body.

'Fuck a duck, Lora King, I got it bad,' she slurs, then as if just noticing it, she lifts the edge of the boa and examines it. 'This belonged to Loretta Young until Wednesday.'

As her arm stretches out, I see a footpath of bruises and welts.

'Lois.'

'These men I know ... they wanted to have a party. I thought it'd just be booze. Sometimes you can't tell. One of them had eyebrows that ran together,' she says, dragging a ragged fingernail across her forehead. 'He looked like out of *Dick Tracy*, you know?'

'Does Alice know you're here?' I ask, remembering what Alice said about telling Lois to stop coming around.

'She told me to come. We ran into each other last night at this place over on Central Avenue, before my date with Big Harry.'

'Who?'

She taps the flaccid skin of her blue-white arm as if in response.

I want to confront her with what is an obvious lie. I want to say, There is no way in the world you saw Alice on Central Avenue. No white woman from Pasadena would– Instead, I say, 'Let me put you in a bath and get some food in you.'

'Bath sounds good. You got any chop suey joints around this neck? I go crazy for chop suey. I think the last thing I ate was a fried bologna sandwich around two o'clock yesterday.'

Her eyes shining like clanging marbles, she laughs as I start to peel the boa from her face.

'Honey, you must really wonder how the hell you got messed up with me.'

Looking in Mike Standish's mirror at 2:00 A.M., my face, neck, shoulders still sharp pink, my legs still shaking, I see something used and dissolute and unflinching. How did this all happen so quickly?

And it has nothing to do with him at all. It is as if this girl in the mirror has slipped down into some dark, wet place all alone and is coming up each time battle-worn but otherwise untouched.

A late dinner at Lido's by the Sea, all cracking seafood, clamoring jazz, squirts of lemon in the air, the clatter of dozens of docked party ships on the water, long strings of lights stretched out into nothing.

Now, back at Mike's apartment, he uncharacteristically down for the count, dreaming heavily, stunned into sleep after a day-into-night of cocktails and courses, a director's wedding, a premiere, a party, and finally dinner with me.

I decide to phone for a taxi.

Tiptoeing into the impeccably tailored dark green and tan tones of the living room, I sit down at the desk, on which rests only a phone, a pad of paper, and a set of fountain pens. I slide open the desk's sole drawer to find a phone book.

As I pull it out, I see that I have inadvertently picked up, along with the phone book, a tidy pack of playing cards. The pack falls soundlessly into the deep carpet. Reaching down, I accidentally knock the cards, and they slide out of the pocket into a near perfect cardsharp's fan.

I kneel on the floor. As I collect the cards wearily, a few flutter again to the carpet, flipping over from the standard navy blue pattern to their reverse sides.

There, instead of the mere jack or diamond, I see slightly grainy, hand-tinted black-and-white photographs.

I bite my lip and faintly recall Bill's army buddies joking about the decks they picked up in France, where, they'd laugh, "women understand men."

The cards are filled with naughty open-legged shots of women, and I avert my eyes, shoving them back into the box. As I do so, however, one catches my eye.

It is two women, wearing only garters, kneeling, hands cupping each other's breasts. Unlike what I had seen in the flash of the other cards, these women are facing not a man just out of frame or their own plump forms. Instead, they look openly into the lens, heavily made-up eyes gazing out.

I stare for a hard thirty seconds before realizing I am looking at Lois Slattery and my sister-in-law.

Lois's unmistakable crooked face.

Alice's brooding eyes – eyes so intense that not even the thick layer of kohl could conceal them, a virtual fingerprint.

They are kneeling on what looks like a cheap Mexican serape.

Their fingernails are painted dark.

They look younger, with a little of the roundness that especially Alice now lacks.

Their mouths are open, Lois's lewdly, like a wound.

Though their bodies and faces are tinted a rosy shade, the photographer hasn't bothered to tint the insides of their mouths, so instead of red or pink, the mouths give way to a gray-blackness like something has crawled inside them and died there. Like their insides have rotted and the outside has yet to catch up.

Suddenly, I hear stirring in the bedroom. Before I know it, I've palmed the card, shoving the rest of the pack back in the drawer.

Mike Standish is standing in front of me, trousers pulled up, suspenders hanging rakishly.

I am still kneeling on the floor, fortunately holding the phone book by way of explanation.

'I'll take you home,' he says with a casual yawn. 'Sorry I fell asleep, King. Bad form.'

'All right,' I say, looking up, knees brushing painfully into the carpet.

He holds his hand out, and I grab it, and as he lifts me to my feet, I feel like the sin could never be greater. Who is this man? And – his hand now casually curved around my lower hip, my buttocks – what have I fallen into, eyes half open or more?

That night I think about the picture of Alice and Lois for a long time. I think about telling Bill. I think about asking Alice. Or Mike. But I know I will do none of these things. I know I will hold on to it, hold on to it tightly. The strangest thing of all is how unsurprising it is. It has a haunting logic. I suppose Alice had been desperate for money. Hadn't she always been desperate for money? How can I know what it was like? I don't know how bad things may have gotten before she had Bill to turn to. I don't even know if the photos were doctored. I don't know anything. But I know I will hold on to the card, tuck it in my drawer under three layers of handkerchiefs, just in case.

Within two weeks, I've banished the thought. After a few awkward encounters, I can finally see Alice again without the image shuddering before me, raw-boned, grimy black and a stark, sweaty white. But I don't forget it.

One weekend, Bill and Alice canceled plans with me at the last minute to go to Ensenada. They came back glowing, brown as café con leche and with a duffel bag filled to bursting with mangoes, melons, passion fruit, ripe and fleshy. Bill pretended to be mad that Alice had snuck the fruit through customs while he, a member of law enforcement, no less, sat beside her. He spoke to her sternly and refused to melt at her lippy pout. But when she made her signature ambrosia dripping with honey and coconut, spelling his name with cherries on top, he ate heartily, pulling her onto his lap and kissing her with a sticky mouth.

A few weeks later, Alice suggests a weekend getaway to Baja, Bill and Alice and Mike Standish and myself.

'You know Bill hasn't quite warmed up to

Mike, and I think this would be a good opportunity for everybody,' Alice says to me in a confiding tone.

'Bill doesn't like Mike?' I say plainly, wondering what she knows.

'I wouldn't say that. I'm sure it's hard for a brother. No man is good enough for his sister, right?'

'It's not as though we're serious,' I say carefully. 'He's just someone I can go out with.'

'All the better.' Alice smiles. 'No pressure, then. Wouldn't it be divine? Swimming, dinner at the waterfront restaurants, dancing.'

'It sounds expensive.'

'Mike can afford it. He's got pockets full of dough.'

'What about Bill?' I say, purposely light.

'Oh, he needs to splurge more. He's too careful. His work is so stressful. It's important that he have fun.'

'I don't know if Mike ... we see each other during the week. I think he has more glamorous commitments during the weekend. I wouldn't feel comfortable asking him.'

'I've already asked him. He wants to go. And don't worry' – she grins at me sidelong – 'I've booked separate rooms for you two, to keep up appearances.'

'Alice,' I say, with a feeling of dread. 'I don't think it's such a good idea.'

'Why not?'

'Many, many reasons. And you *know*.' Because, in truth, I know Bill doesn't like Mike Standish. I can tell by the careful way he speaks about him and to him, or the freighted tones with which he asks, 'How was your evening with the publicity man, Lora? Did he see you home after the party, Lora?' Once I heard him say to Charlie Beauvais, 'What kind of man wears a pink shirt, anyway?' And Charlie laughed, and Bill, rubbing his bristle cut, did not.

'What do I know, Lora?' Alice says blankly but with a faint glimmer in her eyes.

'You know. Let's not go through it all.'

'I don't know what the problem is. I'm suggesting a lovely weekend trip. You should be thanking me,' she says with no apparent guile, only a pretty Alice-smile.

'Bill will not want to do it, Alice.'

'True, at *first*. He didn't want to, at first.' Alice smiles. 'But then he settled down about it.'

And then we are on the highway, in Mike's convertible. Alice is playing Louis Prima loud on the radio and holding her wide-brimmed straw hat to her head, ribbons blowing behind in the breeze. There I am, watching Mike and wondering why we are all here. A cigarette hanging from his mouth, sunglasses shielding his eyes, he smiles lazily at me, as if getting a kick out of the entire improbable thing – what a gas. Here he is with a cop and his schoolmarm sister, two squares who should be sitting on some porch swing in Pasadena, twiddling their thumbs.

It starts with mai tais. We girls are drinking mai tais on the long deck that wraps around the hotel. The sun is setting, burnishing everything, and the rimy drink sets our teeth on edge, and we are leaning back and the drink is churning slowly and warmly inside.

The men have ordered Scotch, which they are nursing quietly. They are trying to find things to talk about. UCLA football. The best way to get to San Diego. Mike's new coupe.

But Alice is skilled at making it work. She beams at Bill and brings up 'topics' and laughs at all Mike's jokes. She tells a long, funny story about a dress she worked on for Greer Garson. She'd had to take it out, and out, and out. They kept sending the dress back, saying the actress was 'er, retaining' and needed more 'room to move.'

Mike has a second Scotch and begins to swap studio gossip, and he places his hand on my leg under the table and it is fine and relaxed.

There is a lengthy discussion about where we should eat and where the best seafood is supposed to be and when is the best time to go.

A sloe-eyed torch singer takes the stage in the bar and begins crooning. Suddenly, there are more mai tais and I notice myself giggling and can't remember why I've begun.

There are two men in panama hats at the table across the aisle who are playing cards.

A trio of couples behind us are arguing raucously about moral rearmament.

A man in the far corner is moving closer and closer to his date, a young Mexican girl who looks uneasy, her thin-slitted eyes darting around.

'Is anybody hungry?' Bill is saying. But the rest of us don't seem to answer, and then there are more drinks and Mike's arm is around my waist, fingers grazing my midriff.

'Don't forget that actor who was sweet on you.' Mike is laughing.

Everyone looks at Alice, who stares blankly.

'Don't you remember? That English fellow who kept saying, "Measure the inseam, darling. The inseam."'

Alice smiles noncommittally, not meeting Bill's gaze.

'Remember how he made you run the tape measure?' Mike chortles, and Alice suddenly laughs, too, despite her efforts. I think maybe I laugh, too.

'I'm glad you don't have to do that

anymore,' Bill says, determinedly lightly.

'They called her the Girl with the Tape.' Mike sighs. 'And they meant it fondly.'

'Oh, Mike,' Alice says dismissively. 'Where should we eat?'

'Let's dance,' I find myself saying, the music from inside swelling sweetly.

'Wonderful!' Alice clasps her hands together. 'Why eat when you can dance?'

'Shouldn't we eat first?' Bill says. 'These drinks must be falling hard on you.'

He is looking at Alice, but it is Mike who laughs. Laughs as if Bill has made a hilarious joke, and turns to me and holds out his hand and I take it. I take it.

And the next thing I know I am pressed against him on the small dance floor, the orange-gold lights of the bar cloaking us, tucking us closely together. The music is so beautiful I think I'll never hear such beautiful music again.

Later, I won't remember what was playing. But I remember one lyric buzzing hot in my ear over and over, 'It was a night filled with ... desperate.'

Later, the lyric won't make sense.

Later, I'll try to remember how it went. But I can't match it. Can't make it work. Can't make the words hang together right.

I'll just remember that we danced and then he seemed to know everything about me and seemed to see everything and he was so limited, such a horribly limited person, but that night he seemed like he knew everything and I would take it. Who was I not to take it?

At just past midnight, Mike deposits me at my door and says good night to us all. My brother and Alice, arms around each other, walk into their room, and I walk into my adjoining one. A few minutes later, I stumble into the shared bathroom. Holding on to the sink, dizzy with drinks and dancing, I laugh at my own reflection, its frenzied gaiety. How has all this happened?

Alice comes in a few minutes later, dress half off, hanging in front of her like a silky bib. I resist the sudden flash before my eyes of her, laid bare, on the dirty playing card. Dizzy with drink, I literally shake my head to knock the image out.

Giggling and hiccuping, she walks toward me, arms out. 'Help me, Lora. Bill's all thumbs.'

Five minutes of giggly fumbling, of her buttons going in and out of distended focus, and I undo her.

She tugs the top half of the dress down to her waist and shakes her arms free, facing the mirror. After a long look at herself, she reaches past me to my cold cream on the counter.

'I always wash the makeup off,' she

stresses, waving past my face. 'No matter how smashed I am. If I can barely stand – if I have to hang on to the sink with one hand to see the mirror – I still do it.'

I nod gravely and watch her scoop the cream with two fingers.

Suddenly, we both hear a knock from my adjoining room.

'Someone's at my door,' I say. Alice's eyes widen. Then narrow.

'Honey, you'd better get it,' she says in a whisper, turning back to her reflection with a faint grin.

'Is it Mike?' I ask as she covers her face in white.

'Go get it, darling,' she says, her red lips still visible. 'I won't tell.'

Vaguely, I want to tell her she has the wrong idea, that I haven't invited Mike Standish back, that I don't know why he might be there, and that there is no secret to keep. Tell whom? But I can't form the sentences. It seems too exhausting. I manage only 'Maybe it's the bellboy ... room service by mistake...'

She keeps looking straight into the mirror, her face a big blank now. I walk back into my room, closing the bathroom door behind me. My left shoe dragging in the carpet, I make it to my room's front door and say, touching the blond wood lightly, 'Who is it?'

'Little Jack Homer,' Mike says.

I open the door partway.

'Is that the one with the thumb and the pie,' I ask.

'Sure, baby.' He reaches a hand from behind him and shows me a bottle of champagne. 'Nightcap, room 411, five minutes or, if you'd like a personal escort, presently.'

When he speaks, his eyebrows rise and his round shoulders tilt forward and I stare at him for a moment, leaning hard against the rough edge of the door, and then I extend my hand without thinking. And I take his arm. And my hand doesn't even seem to make it halfway around its thickness. And his smile is so loose and so easy and only a half smile really, and I don't even stumble because, you see, he wouldn't stumble. He never stumbles at all. And as we walk along the red and tan diamonds on the carpet, the sconces releasing only a soft golden shadow for us, I think this might be all right.

Two hours later, staring up at the shadows of the banana leaves on the ceiling... *This is the end of everything.* The phrase rings out and shoots through the air and quavers tightly, suspended, and does everything but dive into my chest. Could six words ever sound so ominous?

The following night, after a long day at the beach and the markets, we enjoy what becomes a nearly endless dinner on a commercial yacht anchored a few miles from shore. The service is so slow that it is two hours before the food arrives and, along with those at nearly every other occupied table, we become unintentionally fuzzy with drink.

I have never seen my brother drunk before, and he is very charming.

We eat lobster tails and drink champagne, and Mike pays for it all by charging it to the studio. Bill is too softly intoxicated to notice.

Later that night, we end up at an old cantina with Wild West doors. Their feet gliding along the sawdust-covered floors, Mike and Alice dance to a thrumming mariachi band, and Bill and I lean back in rickety chairs and recover from the flush of the dinner.

Somehow, although the music is roaring, we can hear each other perfectly and we recall – together and in impossibly great detail – a favorite Fourth of July from our youth, from the hornet bite on my throbbing leg to the splattery fireworks to the splinters Bill got from skimming along the boat dock as he ran, feet first, into the lake.

–I'm a little drunk, so don't listen to me.

–You're a little drunk, I smile and listen anyway.

–I'm a little drunk, Sis, and feeling like I want to tell you something.

–Anything, I say, chest suddenly, strangely

pulsing, rippling.

–You know, right, even if I don't say it, that I'd do anything for you. Anything.

–I do know, I say slowly, solemnly, so he'll know I mean it.

–We're each other's family and I feel

(His eyes luminous, severe, relentless: saying, Listen to me now because I may never be able to say this again, may never be able to tell you like this what I feel – what I feel and live every day and you do too.)

–I – I'm yours, Sis. You know that, right? I'm all yours and I'm responsible for you and that's what I want.

–I'm glad, Bill

is all I can say, all I know how to say.

He tilts his head against mine, like when children swinging hammock, and gripping hands hard.

And it is there, and happening, and then it is over, gone.

But it breaks my heart it is so beautiful.

I will never forget it.

It is in the middle of that same long, messy summer, before we even know she is pregnant. Amid all the fun, even with its dark edges, Charlie and Edie Beauvais slip unnoticeably off the dance card. We are all too busy to see, to stop for a second. And now, this:

What could be sadder than seeing Edie Beauvais there, white fluffy cloud of hair against the pillow, eyes like two fresh wounds?

I take a long time arranging the lilacs in the vase, unsure what to say.

Her arms lay flat out in front of her, palms facing up, a tissue crumpled in one hand.

'I'm awfully sorry, Edie. I know how much you and Charlie...'

'Hmm,' she says noncommittally, staring out the window.

'If there's anything I can do...'

'Thanks.'

'Would you like me to get you a movie magazine? The new *Photoplay?*' I offer weakly.

She looks over at me without moving or even turning her head.

'Will they let you leave soon?'

'Day or two. I lost a lot of blood. You should have seen it. It was everywhere.'

'I'm sure you'll be back to your old self in no time.' I don't bring up what Charlie has told me, about her not being able to get pregnant again.

Such a little blond thing wasn't meant for this, like wet snow on the pillow, sinking fast and nearly disappearing.

But as I look at her, she all of twenty-three, I wonder what she will do for the next forty years of her life. I know she too is seeing her future spread out before her, years and years of Charlie working long hours and growing older and saggier, and she decorating and redecorating and gardening and going on long drives through the hills and fine lines etching in the corners of her bright eyes and watching other women with their baby carriages and their toddlers and long-lashed schoolchildren and awkward, shiny-faced teenagers and eventually downy, glassy-eyed children of their own. She will have none of this. It will not be hers. And her life feels over at twenty-three. How could one possibly fill those years, days, hours? One sharp slash and her future shriveled up into itself. How could one fill one's life?

This from a man so impeccable. But there it is, in the tipped over bag Mike has left for the laundry, an effluvium of white sheets with a long, hot streak of fuchsia lipstick. I can picture a swirl of candy-colored hair pushed face-first into the bed linen. My stomach turns.

Mike is fast behind me, scooping up the

sheets and shoving them into the bag and yanking it closed with one swift gesture. Like a magician.

I had been about to light a cigarette, even though I don't really smoke. He had already pulled his lighter out of his pocket. And there it is, or was.

I feel something slip inside me, fast and hard, and then suddenly regain its footing before hitting bottom. The shaking hand, cigarette loose between fingers, that had seemed about to move to my face returns instead to my side. Then, a second later, am I really leaning casually against the wall, managing even to finish lighting the cigarette, lifting my head to the still outstretched lighter?

He snaps the lighter shut, looking down at me with watchful eyes. Then, he slides the lighter into his pocket and leans against the wall too.

'Lora King, you continue to surprise me. You really do.'

I look up at him, blowing smoke from behind my lower lip.

He turns his head, appraising.

'I really had you pegged for one of those who would be wrecked.'

I let the smoke fill my lungs, giving shape and texture and spine to the moment. My jaw sets itself, and the warm flush I'd first felt around my eyes, tears waiting to happen, vanishes. I am sucked dry in a heartbeat and feel funny, like I am on strings.

'I thought you'd be a finger pointer, or an hysteric, at least a crier,' he says, not smugly but thoughtfully, like he has just read something unanticipated in the morning paper, something that happened between sundown and sunup.

'Is that the usual routine?' I say, walking toward the center of the room, then turning and facing him again.

'Not always, but with you...' He smiles suddenly and, head still tilted against the wall, he twists around to catch my gaze. 'Aren't I a bastard? Or maybe I'm a powder puff. You see, Lora King, turns out I'm surprising myself this time. Turns out I'm disappointed how little you care.'

I find myself offering a sharp giggle of shock.

'Hard-boiled.' He winces.

Covering my mouth, I concede, 'You're rotten,' before letting the smile spread, blowing smoke. I run the tip of my thumb along my lower lip, brushing away a stray wisp of tobacco.

'Well, then.' He folds his arms and matches my stare, grin-fling like a snake. 'Put out that cigarette, beautiful, and take off the fucking dress.'

It is the middle of August when it happens, when I can't ignore it any longer. It is a postcard of the famous pier, a shadowy couple on the edge, waving in the moonlight. It is lying on the floor of my vestibule. The words 'Welcome to Santa Monica Pier' are punches of light in the sky. The handwriting awkward, as though written from a strange angle or position, or maybe while riding in a car, fast.

Your brothers wife is a tramp, she's no good and she'll rune him. if you dont beleve me, ask at the Red room lounge in Holywd.

I read it over three or four times, squinting at the scratches. There is no postmark. somebody has just slid it under the door. I sit down and read it one more time.

I turn it over, look at the picture again, and then read it even more slowly, studying the address, the turned corner. What could it possibly...

I take a long pause, then pick up the phone. Then put the phone down. Then grab the phone book for Hollywood. Dragging my finger up the page.

Redux Stereophonics

Red Tag Appliances
Red Sam's Pawn
Red Rose Florals
Red Rooster Coffee Shop
Red Room Lounge

Red Room Lounge. 12614 Hollywood Boulevard.

'Hello. I'm trying to find someone. I think she may be a customer.'

'Honey, we're a bar and grill, not an information service.'

'You just might know her name.'

'I don't know names. I don't know nothing. You want a drink, come on by.'

My chest is vibrating. It is six o'clock, or nearly so. If I change and leave immediately, I can be there by seven, but for what? An employee eager to tell me something? A customer? If so, why doesn't the card specify a day and time?

I put the card down and start peeling potatoes for dinner. Soon, however, I begin to feel a tug in the back of my head. Something on the postcard keeps ringing in my ears, but I can't place it. I find myself thinking about Joe Avalon and about the playing card. About many small, taunting whispers in my ear, whispers I'd heard and keep on hearing.

Within fifteen minutes, I find myself in the car, driving toward Hollywood.

Tucked between an Italian restaurant and a peeling office building, the Red Room Lounge is a basic shoe box building distinguished only by a heavily painted crimson door and a chain of paint-spattered lights across the dusty window.

The curtains are pulled across, but as I draw nearer I can see through the gaping edge. There is a mirrored bar, Naugahyde booths, and a few bustling waitresses with red scarves and blank expressions. My hand on the varnished wood handle, I take a breath and walk in.

Youngish to middle-aged men in cheap shirts and flashy grins turn to the door when it shuts behind me, and a few of the dull-faced girls with tightly curled haircuts and painfully arched brows glance over casually.

I guess I must have expected an immediate response, a stranger approaching me, an unmistakable clue. When nothing happens, I find a small table and sit down. A grim-faced waitress with a painfully shorn poodle cut takes my order and brings me a Seven & Seven.

I sit, brushing off the occasional offer of a drink from pointy-jawed scenesters. I sit for nearly two hours, feeling the smoke and grease and desperation fill my pores, wondering what in the world I am doing there, how I happened to fall for this.

'Fuck a duck, it's Big Bill's baby sis.'

It is a long, blue drawl followed by the sharp clack of brightly polished nails on the table in front of me.

I look up: Lois. In all her crooked-faced, ruby-lipped glory.

She sits down, rakishly tugging her tiny evening hat over her eye. Plastic cherries dangle from it, over her shiny white forehead.

'What you doin' here?' she says, dragging the words slowly, looking me up and down amusedly.

'Oh, I don't– I just wanted a drink. I stopped by on my way to meet a friend.'

'Is that a fact? Funny. Don't seem like your type of haunt.'

'It's not really. I just – I didn't know. I...'

Her twisty grin suddenly turns broad and her eyes light up.

'Oh! Oh, I get it. Don't worry, honey. I won't tell.'

'Won't tell what?' I say, my mind racing over what it might mean that Lois is here. Could she have sent the postcard? But if she wanted to tell me something about Alice, why not come right out with it?

'You got a secret admirer,' she murmurs. Then, 'Scotty, another,' pointing to her lipstick-rimmed glass.

'No.'

'A randy-voo. Don't worry, sugar cake. I won't tell.'

'I don't. I just wanted a drink and–'

'And you just thought with your stiff hat and your starched gloves you'd dip into this dive. Don't worry, honey. I'm not bracin' you.'

'Are you here alone?'

'I'm never alone.' She brings the fresh drink to her lips. 'I'm with that party over there.' She points to a corner table filled with raw-boned servicemen and one baby-faced woman whose brightly gartered leg is tucked beneath her, flashing a half mile of creamy, gleaming thigh.

'Friends of yours?' I say.

'Sure.'

Looking over at us furtively, the girl at the table mouths Lois's name. Or at least I assume it's Lois's name. For a split second, I think she's mouthing 'Lora.'

Lois merely waves and turns back to me.

'Who's that girl?' I ask.

'Some gal I met at a casting call. Why? You looking to join the party?'

One of the servicemen slams his glass down, sending ice everywhere. The others laugh even as the girl jumps in her seat, smile stuck on her face. Another grabs her leg and rubs it under the table. Her expression betrays nothing, and he keeps rubbing roughly, eyes fixed on her. A trace of fear skims across her face, but she quickly suppresses it, shifting her leg and slightly shaking herself away, bouncily downing her drink.

She looks back over at Lois fleetingly, eyes jumping anxiously. Lois merely winks back at her.

'No. I ... I wondered if, well, if Alice might have been with you tonight. Do you – Did you ever come here with her?'

'Alice?' Her painted-on brows shoot up and she laughs. 'I don't think so.' So, I realize with something like relief, it isn't Lois who sent the postcard.

She looks over at the increasingly loud, throbbing table of soldiers, then rises, sliding her drink into her other hand, along with her cigarettes and lighter. 'Looks like I should rejoin my party, angel face. Don't miss me much.'

'Okay. Good-bye, Lois.' I hunch my shoulders together, suddenly wishing she wouldn't go. Suddenly afraid for her to go, to join those boys with their hard, tight, coiled hands, shoulders, faces. They look ready to pounce.

She pauses a long, silver moment, looking at me, the comb in her hair glittering in the low lighting. Her smile slides away and she just looks at me, thick, fringy lashes casting shadows across her face. I feel something. I feel something fall away.

And then the smile returns, at its usual half-mast. 'Hey, be careful, peaches. You know?'

'Right,' I say, watching her and watching the servicemen behind her, now all pounding their glasses hard on the table, red-faced and primed. 'You, too.'

She turns, the back of her shiny purple dress sliding after her, swaying like a fish tail, swaying after her as I watch and feel a keen shudder.

I grab my purse, take a sip of my now-watery drink, and stand up. I am out the door before Lois slinks back into that murky red corner.

Later that night, I think about the postcard. Probably just a bitter old boyfriend of Alice's or a romantic rival trying for some measure of revenge. The image of shark-skinned Joe Avalon passes, through my head. Were he and Alice once lovers? One thing feels sure: The writer of the postcard didn't expect that I'd actually go to the Red Room Lounge, figured that the postcard would be enough to stir suspicion. I decide that I'd better forget it.

Three hours of cocktails and crowded dancing in Bill and Alice's living room, their Labor Day party just kicking up at nearly eleven o'clock, a cutthroat game of canasta in the kitchen, an impromptu dance contest on the living room's wall-to-wall, a gang watching a boxing match on the Philco, a bawdy conversation spilling from the powder room into the hallway. And there's my brother standing to the side, looking like a wrung rag, shirtfront wet from crushed rumbas with tireless Alice. He is nearly a foot taller than Alice when she is in her stocking feet, but she exerts so much presence that you never think of the height difference. Bill is always receding into the background, leaning back on the couch, hanging back from the circle gathered in the middle of the party, while Alice looms forward, saucer eyes and manic energy, her red-ringed mouth huge, like a beautiful fish against the glass.

Finally, Mike, an hour late, arrives with an orchid as delicate as a doll wrist.

'My apologies, King. Budding starlet, too much dope, car tipped over half into the canyon. You didn't hear it from me.'

'Can I take your hat?' I hold my hand out.

He smiles, handing me both his hat and his attaché. 'Girl's had a few?'

'It's just the atmosphere. It's like a sponge.'

I walk down the hall to the bedroom and deposit his things on the bed, where a small mound of ridiculously out-of-season fur chubbies and cowls sit. I set his hat on the bedside table and turn around to see Mike standing in the doorway.

'These bulls sure can swing,' he says, as he says many things, as though almost wanting to yawn.

'That they can.' I move toward the door. With a clean gesture, he steps in and shuts the door behind him.

'You are fooling yourself, sir,' I say, 'if you think I would kiss you in my brother's bedroom.'

'Any brother who throws parties like this could hardly care.' He nudges me backward with a thick forefinger. The backs of my legs brush up against the silk coverlet.

'It's Alice's party,' I say, knowing he is playing me.

'Is that how you frame it?' He places the heel of his hand on my collarbone and actually shoves me this time. I fall back onto the bed, the span of furs curling under me, bristling against my neck and arms.

'Tough guy now,' I say, waiting for him to break into his characteristic ironic grin.

140

'That's right.' He looks down at me, no grin.

I feel suddenly hot with shame. All the things that happen in Mike's cool, self-contained apartment start to flash before me.

'Don't–'

His mouth untwists and releases itself into a self-aware smile. 'I'm just kidding, King. You know I have your number. I wouldn't hold it against you.'

I manage a return smile, and take his hand. As I rise, my shoe hits something soft, and my ankle wrenches. We both look down to the floor and see a small steel-blue book slide out from under my foot.

I pick it up and set it back down on the bed.

'I don't think that was on the bed,' Mike says. 'More like under it.'

'No?' I pick it up again, running my finger along the gold edges of the pages.

'See if there's a name in it.'

I open it up and see pages and pages of what appear to be some kind of strange shorthand, all initials and numbers.

'Not another Red,' Mike says.

'It's an address book,' I say, gesturing to the small lettered tabs on the page edges. 'In code.'

'Lots of people don't want their numbers getting around. Especially in this town,' Mike says offhandedly as he opens the door.

'Should I just leave it here?'

Mike shrugs, already halfway out the door, eyes thirsty for a drink.

Suddenly, Alice appears in the doorframe, almost as though she's been hovering just outside of view.

Without knowing why, my heart jumps and I find myself gripping Mike's arm. On instinct, I tuck the address book between the folds of my skirt.

'Look who I find in my bedroom. My, my,' Alice says, shaking her head.

'I was dropping off Mike's hat,' I say.

Alice nods with a teasing smirk. But something in her eyes–

'Where's these drinks I keep hearing about?' Mike says, dropping an arm around each of our shoulders.

'Oh, I see...' Alice laughs with low, raw tones.

Mike laughs too, and we walk together down the hall. We walk with the address book sliding, as if not by my own hand, into my pocket.

Later that night, back at my apartment, I try to steady my party-clogged, smoke-drenched head by lying down. The address book slips out of my pocket onto the bedspread. I pick it up. On the inside cover are the words 'Deau Stationers.' And the tiny address: '312 Hill Street, Los Angeles.' I think about the postcard, trying to see any possible connection.

It isn't the next day, but the day after that I find myself at a small shop with old-fashioned green shutters just around the corner from the funicular railway, that creeps up and down a yellow clay bank from Hill Street. The store looks the part of a once-grand remnant of the sagging, shaggy Bunker Hill neighborhood.

As I walk toward it, I wonder what exactly I am doing. Isn't this likely just some party guest's item, fallen from a coat? But the code is so strange, and the book so fancy, fancier than a schoolteacher or a policeman or any other likely party guest would have. Too ornate for any of those men and too masculine for the women.

I open the door and see a horseshoe glass counter filled with buttery leather-bound books, pale-hued stationery blocks, and sterling silver fountain pens.

A young woman with cat's-eye glasses looks up from her sales sheet.

'Yes?'

I move closer to her, suddenly very self-conscious. What is my plan here?

'I'm wondering if you could help me,' I all but whisper.

'A diary?'

'Pardon?'

She pulls a small, cream-colored leather book from the glass case to her left.

'It has a gold lock and key, gold edging, the most charming gold studs in the tufted padding.' She runs her hand across the top of the book, then looks up at me.

'I ... I don't understand.'

'Oh,' she says, setting the book down. 'Usually I have a good sense about these things. You look like the diary type.'

I feel my face warming. 'Sorry, no. I really just have a question.'

I take the address book from my purse and set it on the counter in front of her. 'Is this from your shop?'

She tilts her head at me and then looks down at the book. She flips the cover open to the stamp on the inner leaf.

'I guess you already knew that,' she says.

My face grows warmer still. 'I do. I guess... I suppose what I'm asking is if you might, somehow, know anything about this purchase. If you might remember making this sale.'

'Do you know how many of these we might sell in a given week?' she asks with a clipped voice, looking back down at the Deau stamp.

'I'm sorry. Of course. Really, I have no idea. Pardon me,' I say, reaching out to

144

retrieve the book.

'We sell less than one in a given week, on average,' she says, holding on to the book with pressed-together forefingers. 'Actually, we sell maybe one or two a year.'

I look up at her.

'It's not a comment on business, which is fair, all things considered,' she continues. 'It's just that this is a custom-made book, sewn with special French thread, hand-pressed leather. We had to order it specially.'

I nod, not seeing.

'This book,' she says, holding it up between two fingers. 'This tiny book costs two hundred and fifty dollars.'

'Two hundred and fifty dollars,' I repeat.

'Yes. This tiny book cost *us* two hundred and fifty dollars when the check bounced.'

'*Oh.*' I see at last.

'Oh indeed. Would you mind telling me how you came upon this book? We'd obviously be very interested in finding its owner.' She holds the book still, despite my unthinking effort to take it back again.

'Don't you know, from the check?'

Pursing her lips, she pulls out a small clipboard from under the counter. To it are attached a few checks and a list of names.

She slides the clipboard toward me, her finger pointing at one of the checks.

'*This* person does not exist. We don't know who passed it.'

It reads, John Davalos.

I feel a wave of disappointment. The name means nothing.

'Ring a bell?'

I say, 'No.'

I say no. But, on a hunch, I take the book from her tight little fingers.

And wish her a fine day. I leave too quickly for her to try to take the book back.

I have the thought it might come in handy.

I do try, at first, to forget about the address book, too. What, after all, do I really know? But it keeps bumping up against me, shoving itself in front of my face like a carnival huckster trailing after you as you hurry past, avoid eye contact, resist the spiel, the hot, fast patter of infinite and gaudy persuasion. Somehow, it lingers with me even more than the dirty playing card. That photo seemed part of Alice's ancient past, but this is Alice's – and Bill's – present.

It is with a vague twitch of guilt that I begin watching her. Before I know it, I find myself watching her everywhere. At Sunday dinner, at social events, at the new school year's first department meetings, I keep waiting to see a connection, a clue. A clue to what, though, really, after all.

There is a string I am pulling together, a string of question marks so long they are beginning to clatter against each other, and loudly.

I count them on my fingers, beginning to feel the fool: the missing credentials, the unexplained absences, the playing card, the postcard, and now the address book. And perhaps most of all, Alice herself. Something in her. The hold so tight over my brother, and suddenly it appears more and more as though she is this brooding darkness lurking around him, creeping toward him, swarming over him. Her glamour like some awful curse.

'Mr. Standish is on set right now. If you'll wait.' The receptionist with the silver fingernails gestures toward a long row of chrome-trimmed leather chairs.

Guests of publicists and press agents don't rate too highly with the front office staff, or so I've come to learn in recent months. I sit down, back straight, as awkward as I always feel anywhere near the studio.

I watch the top of her foamy blond head tilt this way and that as she answers calls on her headset, fingers tapping the ear-pieces with each turn and swivel of her chair.

I look over at a rough-hewn boy seated four chairs down. He has a scar like a lightning bolt over his left eye and wears a sweater and gymnasium shoes.

When he spots me looking at him, he nods, straightening in his seat. Reaching into his pocket, he pulls out a packet of cigarettes, gesturing toward me.

'No. Thank you.'

He nods again and slides one into his mouth. 'Do you mind?'

I shake my head and smile slightly.

Blowing a shallow stream from his mouth, he looks back toward me. 'You in that college movie? The one with all the football scenes?'

'Pardon?'

'Sorry. I just know they're shooting this afternoon and I thought I seen you over there before.'

'No.' I shake my head. 'I'm just visiting someone.'

'I did a few stunts over there,' he says, leaning forward. 'Those pretty boys in the letter sweaters can't take a tackle to save your life.'

I smile. Sensing he expects a reply, I say, 'Did you get that scar from doing stunts?'

He touches his forehead self-consciously, and I feel bad. I assumed he'd be proud of it, like a battle wound.

'No, I got this a long time ago. Old bar

fight. But I've been working here for a while now.'

He looks at me expectantly, and I can tell he is waiting for a response.

'How did you get into stunt work?' I offer, hoping Mike will show up.

'Oh, I was knocking around, trying to find a way to make some money for taking punches, rather than taking them for free,' he says. It sounds like he's said it many times before, to great effect.

I try to stop the conversation politely with a closing smile.

'I been doing it for four years now.'

He takes another drag. 'I did a stunt for Alan Ladd once. Frank Sinatra even.'

'Well, well.'

Suddenly, the foamy blond head of the receptionist pops up, and her nasal voice rings out, 'Teddy, Mr. Schor is through with him. Mr. Davalos is on his way out. He wants you to bring the car around.'

The boy jumps up, suddenly flustered.

'On it,' he shouts, dancing on the balls of his feet for a second before nodding his head toward me and heading to the door.

Mr. Davalos. Suddenly, I see the arched brow of the woman at Deau Stationers as if she were right before my eyes. Mr. Davalos. Could this be the owner of the address book in my sister-in-law's bed? No. I must have misheard. The name has occupied my thoughts so much in the last few days that I must have imagined hearing it aloud.

I take the opportunity to pick up a *Modern Screen,* in case the boy returns and wants to continue the conversation. Burying my head behind it, I wonder how long Mike will be and if I should really keep waiting.

A few minutes pass before I hear a quiet, faintly familiar voice. 'Is Teddy out there?'

'Yes, Mr. Davalos. He should be waiting for you.'

'Thank you.'

As the voice trails away, I glance up from the magazine just in time to see Joe Avalon, resplendent in sharkskin, passing the reception desk and through the office doors.

He doesn't see me.

I rise as he steps out. Walking to the window, my heart jumping a bit, I look out. Tugging his hat down, he opens the door of a sleek black roadster. I see a flash of deep maroon interior as he pulls the door shut behind him and the car leaps to life and drives off.

Joe Avalon is John Davalos.

Shaken out of my shock by the nervous buzzing at the reception desk, I turn around on my heel, almost losing my balance.

Foamy-head is watching me. 'Mr. Standish says he's coming.'

'Fine,' I say. Ticking my finger lightly on the window, I ask, 'Who was that man? I

150

think I know him.'

She pauses and looks at me for a moment. 'That's Mr. Davalos.'

'Does he work for the studio?'

She pauses again. 'He's not a casting agent, if that's what you mean.'

'No, no.' I smile. 'I'm not an actress. I just think I've met him before.'

I then add, 'Maybe through Mr. Standish.'

'He doesn't work here. He's a business associate of Mr. Schor's.'

'I see,' I say, just as Mike pushes open the glass doors.

'Let's go, doll,' he says, tipping the hat in his hand to Foamy-head. 'Before the gray fellows call me back. I gotta talk to a few columnists at Sugie's.'

Joe Avalon. What more do you need, I ask myself. What more do you need to know you must do something? The next morning, as Alice gathers her sewing samples for our first day back to school, I grab her phone book and pass through it as quickly as I can. I'm not sure which number is his. There is nothing under A or D that fits. I end up looking under J, and there is a number without a name attached. In my haste, I end up scribbling it on the inside of my wrist.

That afternoon, during my prep period, I call the operator, who tells me that the name listed with the number is J. Devlin. Given the multiplying names, I feel sure that it's Joe Avalon. And then, she actually gives me the address. As I write it down, I wonder what exactly I think I'm going to do. But something keeps telling me I've waited long enough, let enough strange glimmers accumulate in the corners of my eyes. It's time to stop blinking.

After dropping off Alice after school, I drive into Los Angeles and find the house on Flower Street. I sit in my car for three hours, and he never appears.

I go back the following evening. I sit and watch. I think about Bill. I think about Joe Avalon in my brother's bedroom. I think about Alice and what she has brought with her, what she's carried into my brother's world. Our world.

At a little past ten, a car pulls up his driveway. I duck down in my seat and then wait, watch.

Joe Avalon, in a shiny raincoat, emerges and heads for his front door. I ask myself, Could this man really be Alice's lover? And if not that, what?

He is alone. Here is the opportunity. There is no reason to wait. I banish the strumming refrain in my head. The one that keeps asking what I think I'm doing here, after all.

As he unlocks his door and walks inside, I slide out of my car and walk to his house. There is no use thinking about it, I just have to do it, without thinking, just go...

I am suddenly there, knuckles rapping the pine door.

And it's a long minute before he opens it, coat off, collar open, blast of cologne in my face. He doesn't know what to make of it.

'Miss King, right?'

He opens the door wider. 'Come in,' he says. He says, 'Come in.'

I step past him and into the darkly paneled hallway of the pristine, cocoa-colored bungalow.

'I can't guess why I'm so lucky,' he says softly. He always speaks softly, and low, so you have to lean in to hear. A trick like a southern belle's.

The hallway spills into a living room, Oriental rug, teak-colored blinds, amber lamps, and a large, plush sofa in deep rose.

'Have a seat.' He buttons his collar, twisting his neck. 'Can I get you a drink?'

I shake my head, but he begins pouring two glasses from the mahogany bar cart. Whiskey and two quick sprays of soda from a smooth green bottle.

He hands the drink to me and gestures for me to sit on one of the damask chairs. Opposite me, he settles on the sofa. My hand curls around the glass, and I'm suddenly glad I have it to hold on to. I finally look at him straight on. I can't avoid it. His eyes, glossy dark like brine, fixed and waiting.

'I couldn't be more surprised, Miss King. I'm sitting here thinking that I don't even know how you know where I live. Is this about our mutual friend Alice?' He says this all nearly tonelessly, only the vague lilt of someone very conscious of how he speaks, the words he wants to use.

'I have something of yours.' This is what I say. I just say it, and that's it.

'Is that right?' he shoots back more quickly than I anticipated.

'I have something of yours.' I look him straight in the eye this time, and his right lid twitches for just a second.

'And what is that, Miss King?'

'You can't guess?' I watch his face. I want him to admit something, confess to something, betray something.

'Miss King, I really can't imagine.' He smiles vaguely, unreadably. 'But I'd really like to know.'

'I bet you would.' How I manage to say this, I don't know. *It's like a movie scene. This is what they say in the movies.*

'This could go on forever, Miss King.' He slouches back in his seat. 'Do you have a direction in mind for this exchange?'

I open my purse and pull out the address

book, keeping it close to my chest.

He looks at the book and doesn't flinch.

'Do you want it back?'

'That's supposed to be mine?' He gestures toward it.

'I know it's yours.'

'Let me see it. I'll tell you if it's mine.' He looks down at me, not making a move.

'It's yours, but that's not the interesting part.' I feel a strange bravado lurching up in my chest. I can't guess where it's coming from.

'I'm waiting, Miss King. Don't think I'm not curious.'

'I found it in my sister-in-law's bed,' I say squarely.

He pauses and manages a slight grin. *That's* the interesting part?'

'How did it get there?'

He leans back, setting his glass on his knee and spreading his arms along the back of the sofa.

'This is about your brother's wife. This is about you wanting to pin something on your brother's wife.' He can't hide a smile.

'No. No,' I say, reacting instantly to the strange allegation. What does he mean? What could he possibly mean? 'I'm just trying to find out what...'

My mouth inexplicably goes dry. Pin something on my brother's wife? *Why would I...*

I hear some sound come from within me. My jaw begins shaking suddenly. It seems to be rattling.

He takes a sip from his drink, smile still suspended there. The glass has left a faint ring on the knee of his cream-colored pants. I stare at it, trying to regain my focus.

'I just want to know...' It's hard to talk with my jaw doing this. I can't make the words sound smooth.

He raises his eyebrows expectantly, waiting for me to finish my sentence.

'...what it was doing there. I just want to know...'

I wonder, can he hear that? Can he hear how loud my jaw is? It seems so loud I can barely hear myself. A horrible rattling like a dying snake.

'Why didn't you ask your sister-in-law?' He smacks his lips ever so slightly, holding the glass with its still popping soda water. 'Why don't you?'

'Maybe I did,' I blurt, fixing my hand on my jaw to keep it in place.

'I don't think so.' He smiles.

'No. I... I just want for you to tell me. I didn't want...' It's hard to answer because I don't know what the answer could be. To tell the truth, I'd never even thought to ask Alice. To tell the truth, it is as if, lately, as everything keeps surging forward, it is as if I am seeing her through glass, through dark water three feet deep.

'You wanted something over her?' he says, tilting his head.

He watches me squirm and shake my head fervently, but then his smile slips away for a moment, as if he has just realized something.

'How did you know it was mine, anyway?' My jaw finally settles a bit. If I clench it, I can speak.

'That doesn't matter,' I say.

'I might decide that.' His voice turns cooler. 'You'd better just spill it all, Miss King.'

Then he says, 'You, honest, don't know what you're getting yourself into.'

Then he says, 'And I think you better give me the fucking book.'

Then, finally, 'It's mine, after all.'

I stand up, my drink nearly slipping from between my fingers as I press the book to my chest. I feel foolish. If he really wants it, my little grasp isn't going to stop him.

I set the glass down.

Things suddenly feel far more complicated.

And all the reasons for not bringing the book with me, much less coming at all, swirl through my head. I wonder exactly what I am doing here.

I turn on my heel, intending, I suppose, to get as far as I can. Thinking, I guess, that it would be too embarrassing for him to overpower a woman.

But then thinking he might overpower a woman every day.

I can feel him watching me for a moment, then I see him, from the corner of my eye as I begin to walk to the door, calculatedly break into a shrug.

'You want it, you got it, Miss King,' he says, standing, his thin-lipped smile hanging from one side of his face.

Then he adds, 'I don't need it.'

And finally, 'It's been more than an even trade.'

I open the door, and my hand is shaking like a string pulled taut and plucked hard.

On the drive home, my jaw buzzes, hums, nearly sings. I jam the heel of my hand underneath it, steer with one hand, and turn the radio as loud as it will go. The zing of the brutish jazz finally vibrates hard enough to drown it out.

My head clogged with incomplete revelation after revelation, I avoid Bill entirely. Any other time, he would be the one I would go to, would have long gone to, for help. But this time I can't.

Instead, the next night, unable to sleep, I end up at Mike Standish's apartment.

'You're awful dirty, Lora King. I wonder if anybody has any idea what a dirty girl you are.'

I don't answer, don't like him saying it, even if I am curled against the edge of his bed, my knees on the floor, persuaded not to put my stockings on, persuaded to stay right where I am and look up at him, straight into his laughing eyes.

I sit there and I try to frame a question. But I can't.

'I'm going home.'

'Why go home? No one's keeping tabs on you. Come on.'

'You don't need me to stay.' I reach for my stockings, pull them slowly from the tangle of sheets.

'I do.' He sighs, stretching his arms above his head. 'I really do.'

'You like to sleep alone.'

He seems – it is dark and hard to tell – to smirk a little before he says, 'I think you should stay. You are the one I like to stay.'

I almost ask why and then I don't ask why and my stocking, via my own slightly trembling hands, is streaming up my leg.

'Come on. I like you here and I like the way you smell. I like making you stay.' He yawns.

Here he is, the man who knows things and

who should want to help me. But it is so hard to bring up things with any weight at all to a man like this. A man like this doesn't have real conversations.

He is lying there whistling contentedly, and I just close my eyes. For weeks, I've been deciding whether to ask him, ask him anything about what I've learned, or almost learned. Now, with what I have seen, with Joe Avalon and more and more questions, it seems I don't have anything to lose.

'I saw some pictures, Mike,' I say, biting my lip a little, snapping my belt, adjusting my collar, feeling the need to straighten myself.

'It's all about pictures, King. Don't you forget it. It's my bread and butter.' He reaches over and touches my belt lightly with a finger, leaning in and sending a shot of peppery cologne to my face.

'I mean specific pictures. Bad ones. Here in your apartment.' I look at my gray shoes, pointy-toed and confident. Teacher shoes.

'I got pictures like that, sure,' he says, and I realize, with regret, that he is scrambling, dancing.

'Pictures on playing cards. One of them, it was of my sister-in-law. Of my brother's wife. And Lois Slattery.'

He smiles. He nearly grins, but it's an effort. 'Oh, right. Yeah, I really didn't want you to see that. Not – not because... Frankly,

King, I thought it would hurt you.' The voice almost soft. 'Because of your brother.'

I can barely stand it. I honestly feel my knees buckle. There he is, this cold, rather limited man with – is it? – a distinct look of kindness in his eyes.

'How did you get those pictures?' I manage, recovering.

'Lora...' He sighs and sinks back into the bed.

'Tell me where you got those pictures.'

'Listen ... listen, we live differently, in different worlds. Truly, Lora, your world, your world is kind of beautiful. Why bring my world into it? Why–'

'Tell me, Mike. You'd better tell me.' I look down at him.

'She gave them to me,' he says, firmly, deliberately, but unable to look me in the eye for long. 'To show me. She wanted me to see, Lora. She wanted me to see.'

Later that night I lie in bed and think about what he said and how far I was able to push him and the point at which I couldn't ask any more questions. *Wanted you to see what?* I wanted to ask, but didn't. *And did you? Did you see what she wanted to show you?* Somehow I knew he had and now I had, too.

As the days pass, there is nothing else I can think about. I'm not sure when my suspicions about Alice slipped from the ambiguous to this, to an instinctive desire to know, to know what had found its way into our family, our life. But it happened, and not a few days later, I am back at Joe Avalon's neighborhood and then at his house.

I sit in the car, with *Photoplay, Look,* anything they had at the drugstore, knowing it could be hours before I see anything, if I see anything at all. I feel like Girl Detective from the serials, my Scotch plaid thermos filled with black coffee, a scarf over my head. Am I close enough? Am I far enough away? What if I do see something? Would I know what to do? Could I follow another car, if I needed to? What if I were spotted, what then?

It doesn't take hours, only forty-five minutes. The door to Avalon's bungalow opens, and I am watching as it happens. I see the pine green door open and see the woman come out with Joe Avalon's hand delicately on her back. With a quick verbal exchange, he disappears back into the house. The woman walks down the small path to the street, down the sidewalk, and on. Her gait is slow, strange, dreamy.

Although she is on the other side of the street, she is moving hazily in my direction, and I duck quickly as she walks past. Then, I turn around and get a better look as she continues her slow way down the street. She wears a navy and white suit, and a white hat with a large brim. Her handbag swings neatly, a fine circle of white patent leather hanging from her arm. A purchase from Bullock's that ran her nearly forty dollars.

I know because she told me soon after she bought it. I know because it is Edie Beauvais sashaying out of Joe Avalon's house and down Flower Street.

At a safe distance, I start the car and turn it around, moving slowly. Inching along, I watch her reach her own car, parked three blocks away.

I wonder how in the world Edie Beauvais could come to know Joe Avalon. Edie Beauvais, whom everyone knew was still suffering from 'the blues' after her summer miscarriage, Edie Beauvais, cop's wife. I don't wonder for long: the only possible link between this Pasadena housewife and this Los Angeles shark is Alice.

As she drives away, I follow her as discreetly as I know how for several miles, until it becomes clear to me that she has no destination. She takes me high into the hills and then down again, and finally straight to the ocean. As I drive, I consider whether Joe Avalon is Alice's lover or Edie's. Or how it came to be that Alice introduced the two.

I keep telling myself that she must notice me. There are too few cars on the road, it has gone on too long. But I can't stop myself. I follow until she finally pulls into the lot of a stucco establishment with a sign twice as big as the place itself: 'Recovery Room Inn.' Apparently so named because a rundown charity hospital is across the street.

I know I can't follow her inside. The place is too small. So I wait. This time for two hours.

It is nearly eight o'clock when she emerges, hat in hand, hair blowing in the breeze, pink smile wide as she chats with a tall man in a gray suit and a dark woman with the kind of high-topped veiled hat popular ten years ago. Well past tipsy, Edie and the man laugh heartily, hands to bellies. The veiled woman lights a cigarette and throws the empty pack into the street, tapping her shoe as if ready to go.

They wind their way to Edie's car, and the man gets in the backseat, and the woman sits beside Edie, who keeps laughing, hands on the steering wheel. At last, as the woman smokes long, slow, flat clouds, Edie starts the car.

It is getting dark, and I'm not sure how

long I'll be able to follow, but I figure I'll try. It requires all my attention as Edie's car weaves and meanders and keeps accelerating and then slowing unexpectedly.

Finally, Edie stops at a bungalow court on Pico Boulevard. The lot is too small for me to enter unnoticed, but by parking on the street out front I can see into the courtyard through its overhanging arch. All three suddenly appear underneath it and then seem to turn into one of the apartments.

I wait a moment and get out of my car. Walking over to the floored patio, I step under the arch and see a dozen apartments laid out in a rectangle. Along one side there are a series of mailboxes. I look over in the direction the trio walked and guess they entered either Apartment 3 or Apartment 5.

Then I move over to the mailboxes for a closer look. Apartment 3 has the name Chambers listed and Apartment 5 has the name Porter written in unconfident pencil.

Suddenly, the door marked 5 begins to open. Frantic for some excuse for my loitering, I remember in a flash that I have Alice's cigarettes still with me from a few weeks before, when her clutch was too small to hold them. Plucking the pack out, I fumble one to my mouth. Swiveling a little, I make large gestures of trying to look further into my purse.

The man from the car emerges from the

apartment. He wears a tan suit, and his skin is very pale and looks clammy. He stands a moment and wipes his cheeks with a handkerchief.

Still stalling, I nearly shake the contents of my purse to the ground, pretending to be looking for a lighter or matches. This is a mistake.

'You need a light?'

I turn to him. He looks about thirty years old, with hair prematurely steel-edged. I try to fix his face in my mind, but there is little to hold on to: pencil-thin mustache, weak chin, twitching, blinking eyes.

'Yes, thank you.'

We move toward each other, he with an extended hand. He holds a gold-colored lighter under my nose and flicks it. I puff anxiously, having smoked perhaps a dozen cigarettes in my life.

'You live here?' he asks.

I begin walking away. 'I was just visiting a friend.'

The thought that Edie might, at any minute, step outside, keeps flashing through my head.

He nods. 'Me, too. I just needed some air. These apartments are sweatboxes.'

'Thanks for the light,' I say, backing away a bit.

'We're having a party in that apartment,' he says, waving his handkerchief at the door.

'You know?'

He looks at me levelly. 'Maybe you'd like to join us.'

'No, no.' I back myself nearly to the mailboxes, my elbow hitting one metal box hard.

'Sorry,' he says evenly, with a shrug. 'I thought you were ... someone else.'

'Someone else?'

'Never mind.' He shakes his head. 'I got it wrong.'

He offers a tilted head and a grin, and then I watch as he opens the door, disappearing inside.

It is at this moment that I realize I am smoking so deeply my throat feels raw, thick with tar. By the time I get to my car, I have finished the cigarette and feel my stomach turn. There is this sense that the closer I come the more things slip away.

I sit in front of the wheel for maybe fifteen minutes, trying to explain things to myself. Edie. Joe Avalon. Alice. What kind of sticky web connects these three? I drive around the block a half dozen times. Then I park back in the lot and get out of the car again, not sure what I am going to do.

I find myself approaching Apartment 5 again with a sick feeling in my stomach.

I decide to walk behind the building into the wide alley. Overcome by the mingling smells of ripe garbage and heavy jasmine, I put my hand over my nose. There is a white apartment number painted on each overflowing trash can, and I quickly locate Number 5. There is one small window facing the alley. I walk over to it, conscious of every small tap and scuffle my shoes make.

I peer in between the shutter slats, seemingly drunk on my own sense of invisibility.

I can't see much, but I can see this.

I can see Edie, her whipped cream hair piled high on top of her head, sitting on the edge of a bathtub wearing a half-slip and stockings. Her hands cover her face, but I know it is her.

At first I think she has a scarf tied jauntily around her upper arm.

And then, feeling foolish, I realize.

This, of course, is what could bring together a vulnerable Pasadena housewife and a Los Angeles shark. If nothing else, this.

If there's a way to describe it, it's like the world, once sealed so tight and exact, has fallen open – no, been cracked open, and inside, inside...

I am ready to tell him, to tell Bill. To tell him at least what I have seen, if not the lengths I've gone to see it.

Even if I don't know what the clues point to, the clues themselves are troubling enough. Joe Avalon in his home, his bed-room. Edie Beauvais. God, does Charlie know? Shouldn't Charlie know? I tell myself it is Bill's job to string clues like this together. I can, as tenderly as possible, give him the clues, and he can see what they add up to. As hard as it will be for him to hear, I have to tell.

That night, Alice suggests an evening out at a dark-walled Latin dance club.

At first, I decline her invitation. But, knowing how hard it is to get Bill alone anymore and knowing Alice will be the one dancing while Bill will mostly sit and watch, nursing one watery drink for the entire evening, I decide to go.

As I sit there with him in the curved booth, however, I am frozen. How do I say these things to him? I try to imagine how he would tell me.

'Sis,' he says, head turned, hand lightly on my forearm. I can't look into those eyes. I look down instead at the slightly dented knuckles on his cop hands. When he was on the beat, they'd often be grated raw across the joints from rough arrests, from holding men down while his partner cuffed them, from climbing fire escapes and breaking up bar fights and dragging drunks through cracked doorways.

His hands are smoother now but still studded with small, healed-over tears, flecks of white from old scars, old stories mapped onto him, some stories he won't tell even me.

His hand rests on my arm. 'Sis.'

'Yes.' I manage a sidelong glance at his sharp, focused eyes.

'How are things?'

'Fine, Bill.'

'You like this Standish guy, huh?' The familiar strain to sound casual. Even after all these months, Bill still turns away, teeth clenched, when he sees Mike with his hand on me.

'He's fine. That's all. You know.' *This is what we do.*

He shrugs a little, softening. 'Well, Alice says he's okay, so.'

'She should know,' I say. *I have to do it now. Now.*

As if on cue, Alice flits by on the dance floor, bottle green dress throbbing, a man with a pencil-thin mustache leading, but just barely.

'Doesn't that bother you?' I say. 'Her dancing with other men?'

'No, I like it,' he blurts out, eyes fixed on her until she slips out of sight. 'I mean, she enjoys it,' he quickly adds with a shy smile. 'I'm no match. I can't keep up with her.'

His eyes tracing her, sparking with energy. *No I like it. This is my wife. Look at her. Christ would you look.*

Is there no end to the devotion? What dark corners would it furrow around and where would it end? What are its limits?

'You know what Charlie said to me,' Bill says. 'He said, Billy, you couldn't have dreamed up a wife like that.'

'Yes, Bill.' I steal another look, and I see he's glowing. He's nearly red-faced with — what is it? Pride.

'She's very special, Bill,' I add. A sharp pain, my own nails into the heel of my own hand. What am I waiting for?

'I remember, on our honeymoon...'

He can't possibly–

'Sis, she was so beautiful it hurt to look. On the beach, hand over her eyes, looking out on the water and talking gentle and low, dizzy from the sun, talking about how I'd changed everything for her.'

'You did.' I nod.

'I must be going soft from that last drink,' he apologizes with a grin, tapping his fingers lightly on my arm.

'No, I know.' I'm ready. I am.

Lost in his own thoughts, he turns his face away from me suddenly. Then, 'Lora, I do know she's not like the other girls. Like Margie, Kathleen ... I know she's not like them. But...'

He knows. He knows she's something foreign. Something not us. He tilts his head thoughtfully. 'She's been knocked around a little. And I've seen, from the job, what that can do. I know what that can do to a girl. Even the best girls.'

He looks at me, his face lit by the candle on the table. His eyes darken a little. I see it.

Then, decisively, he thrums two fingers on the table. 'But it hasn't done it to her. She fought it off. And, really, isn't that something?'

He smiles, waiting for me. For my reassurance.

'Bill.' I can't bear it. I put my other hand on his. 'I want–'

Then, just as he is about to lean toward me, to hear what I am saying, he spots Alice again on the dance floor.

I can see his eyes catch, lock. I can see a change sweep hard over his face.

She is looking at him. She's dancing with some man, any man, and looking at my brother. Her eyes like black flowers. She places one white hand across her collarbone, her mouth blood red. It's so open, so bare, I can't look.

How could she know? But she does. She knows and she's watching, waiting, marking time, seeing what I will do. And then Bill

He is rapt. He is mesmerized.

It's like this: she's on the dance floor, eyes tunneling into him, and then she's in front of him, right next to me, crushed satin skirt skimming my own legs as she presses toward him, leans down with that great gash of a mouth, and with one long finger under his upright, always upright chin, she kisses him with her whole charged little body. So close I can feel my brother shudder.

And then, before he – or I – can take a breath, she has disappeared back onto the swarming dance floor.

One hand on my stomach, I feel strangely sick.

This is when I realize there are some things you can't tell.

This is when I realize:

He wouldn't tell me at all. He'd just make it go away.

I know what I have to do.

That night, desperate to forget for a while, I call Mike. I don't tell him about anything that has happened, especially not about seeing Edie Beauvais. But something in my voice, he hears something in my voice that makes him know he should say: 'Tonight I'm taking you out of this burg.'

When I get in his car, he smiles. 'Hey, kid. We're going to the Magic Lamp.'

And before I know it we are on Route 66, and we keep going and we pass the Derby and the Magic Lamp and suddenly we are deep in the desert.

Light breaking up in the clouds as dusk gives over, and we're driving and we're driving and it seems we'll never get anywhere, but with my hands resting in the creamy folds of my dress and with the sound of Mike faintly tapping fingers on the leather steering wheel as the music burns off us both, as the radio sounds not tinny but like a movie score streaming over us, like in a movie, like a movie where they're driving and the red dusk envelops them in gorgeously fake rear screen projection, the car jumping not like real cars but like movie cars, carrying you away with the lush romanticism of the night, the sharp jaw-line of the leading man, the soft curls of the ingenue who has all the promise of turning siren or vamp by the night's end.

It is that evening that he tells me, after rounds and rounds of drinks in a far-off roadhouse, leaning over and whispering into my ear, the thing he couldn't bring himself to tell me before. I know, even as my own head is swirling, that he will regret telling me this. Even Mike Standish sometimes slips. But he does tell me. And the whole ride home, I feel sick with it.

He tells me this:

Time was, a few months back, he couldn't believe what he'd gotten himself into. Yes, he'd had a few jaunty turns on his mattress with costume girl Alice Steele, he'd admit it. But who'd have guessed a year or so later she'd ask him to take out the schoolteacher sister of her new cop husband?

Truth was, he'd done it as a favor, but he'd never liked Alice all that much. She spooked him with her heavy eyes and the strange stories he'd heard.

He remembers seeing her once in a colored nightclub on Central Avenue. He knew why *he* was there. A fast detour, giving a dark-meat-loving matinee idol a guided tour of the city's murkier regions. But Alice, she was in the middle of everything, her stark white face looming out from a crowd of colored jazz musicians and one slick-faced white man puffing hard on a reefer. She wore a low-cut velvet dress hanging by two long strings off her shoulders, and her mouth was like one gorgeous scar across her face. He remembers thinking she looked as though she might slide out of that dress and slither across the floor, and caught by the image, he found himself inexplicably terrified. Then, feeling embarrassed and foolish, he recovered. He waved over at her, he sent her a drink.

She stared at him with eyes like bullet holes, stared at him like she'd never seen him before, and he felt his blood pulsing, the vein in his neck singing. She wasn't just a B-girl, she was carrying the whole ugly world in her eyes.

Two hours later he had talked her into the alley and he'd had her for the fourth and last time since he'd met her, and hands so hard on her white thighs that he thought his fingers might meet right through her, he knew he could never see her again.

He did, but never like that.

The next time he saw her she was married to a cop and wore a scratchy wool suit and sensible pumps.

And her new sister was set out for him like fresh meat.

I avoid Bill all week, unable to face him. It is not until the following Sunday that I drive over to his house for a twice-postponed dinner. My chest surges as I walk in and see him sitting on the sofa with his head in his hands.

'What is it? Is Alice–'

At that moment, Alice walks into the room with a brandy. She hands it to Bill, placing her hand gently on my back.

'Did he tell you?' Alice gives me a heavy stare.

'Tell me what?' I sit down beside him and touch his arm.

'Edie Beauvais. She's dead.'

'What?' I feel my voice shake. I saw her just over a week ago. Even if she didn't see me.

Bill raises his head, face flushed, and looks at me. 'She killed herself with pills. Can you believe it?'

'No,' I say. 'I can't.'

'The miscarriage and everything.' Alice sighs. 'I think she felt everything had turned bad for her.'

'It can't be,' Bill says. 'Poor Charlie.'

I try to figure it, try to figure this into what I saw. I want to watch Alice closely, to see what she might know. Does she know all that I do, or much more? Does she know how far Edie Beauvais had gone? Had she watched her go?

But all I can focus on is Bill's wrecked face.

'We'll go see him, Bill. We'll bring him dinner. Be with him,' I say, thinking of how much Bill relies on Charlie, his only real friend. And, ever since Bill married Alice, there has been that special closeness between them, both always watching their lovely, baffling wives from the sidelines, perpetually bemused and lovestruck. Always, I realize now with a wince, always so many steps behind.

'He's gone,' Alice says. 'He left the hospital and got in his car, and Bill hasn't been able to reach him.'

177

'I was at the morgue with him,' Bill mumbles, clenching the table edge with his hands, almost wringing it. 'He didn't really seem to react at all. And then suddenly he bolted out of there. I tried to follow him, but he just took off. I don't know where he could be.'

Sitting beside him, I place my hand on his back. He grabs my fingers, tugging at them. We sit that way for several minutes. I wonder if Bill is thinking what I am: that there might be some lesson one should draw from this, from what happened to his friend. About the price one, might pay for a love so crushing and for a woman so filled with secrets.

It reminds me of a conversation I witnessed between Bill and Alice right after Edie's miscarriage. Bill had talked about how these women, they were so delicate, like those flowers that look too heavy for their stems to support, that seem to defy their very structures.

'I'd say you men are the fragile ones,' Alice had replied. 'Too soft for this world.'

When she said it, I thought she was teasing, but I could tell Bill was affected, that he found the remark surprising, penetrating. Even if he couldn't quite put his finger on why.

The look in Bill's eyes had been: *She knows things. Things I can't begin to know.*

As I remember it now, with my hand on Bill's shoulder, I lift my eyes to see Alice standing there, her face a hieroglyphic.

'Is Alice there, honey?'

I know it is Lois on the phone, but it is Lois even more slowed down than usual, her voice dragging by its hind legs, barely making it from her lips to my ears.

'She'll be back around eight. She's gone downtown to buy some fabric – in Chinatown, I think.' I had stopped by hoping to see Bill, to console him. But he was gone, too, working late again.

'Oh, God ... for real? Is she going to be home soon?'

'Not until about eight,' I repeat. 'Is everything all right, Lois?'

'Don't even ask ... that creep. That son of a bitch. I can't even believe... Can you... So she's downtown, huh? She's... I'm in Culver City, I think. I don't even know.'

The eerie, wavering pitch of her voice unnerves me. Shivery like a zither in a monster movie. She sounds as if she can scarcely hold on to the phone, barely make the words come out of her mouth.

'Is there anything I can do, Lois?' I find

myself asking. 'Sleep tight, baby. Sleep tight, let's call it a day,' she murmurs, half-singing.

'What were you calling Alice for?' I say. 'Did you need some help? Is everything okay?'

There is a pause, a faint sound of contorted humming, then a clicking sound, like a drawer sliding on its runners, open and shut.

'Lois?'

I clutch the receiver as my stomach rises anxiously into my chest. I get a sudden feeling of monumentality. I whisper one more time, hardly a whisper even, 'Lois, are you there?'

'Yeah?' she says at last. I take a breath.

'Lois, why don't you tell me where you are and I can come get you and bring you over here?' I can't believe I'm saying it. But if not me, who would go? Who would go?

'Me? I'm on a fast track to nowhere, baby,' she says, then laughs lightly. Then, suddenly, 'Would you come by? Would you?'

Then, 'God's honest, I'm afraid he's gonna come back, and he said if he did he'd bring the pliers this time.'

The car keys I've unconsciously palmed drop to the floor with a clatter and I nearly lose the phone. Breathing deeply, I force out, 'Tell me where you are, please. Please tell me' – and I am suddenly half out of breath – 'where you are.'

The Rest E-Z Motel in Culver City. I drive by it three times, hands tight on the steering wheel, trying to steel myself. On the phone, Lois said she didn't know what room she was in. She said she couldn't get up to look at the door. I will have to try to find her by talking to the clerk.

The place looks about as I had guessed when she told me its name. The shaggy carport leading to the, lobby hanging so low it seems nearly to hit the tops of the stray cars that move underneath. Gray shingles cracked in the sun, and bloodred trim caked around each window and awning of the dozen or so rooms.

My legs shake as I walk across the parking lot. It doesn't strike me until that moment that there is every reason to believe this sort of thing happens to Lois five times a week and she emerges each time with only her usual number of scratches.

The clerk, a Mexican with a cigarillo and a bowling shirt, looks me over dubiously from behind a grimy counter. He scratches the back of his neck.

'Hello. I'm looking for a friend. She called me from here, but she was ill and wasn't sure which room she was in.'

He blinks slowly and raps his fingers on the counter.

'She's small, maybe five feet two or so,

with dark hair.' I gesture with my hand.

His lips twist around the cigarillo. His fingers rap more slowly, and he shakes his head.

I open my purse, hands shaking slightly. 'I'd be so grateful for any help you can give.'

He shakes his head again, raising his hand to me.

'Really.' I slide ten dollars across the counter, Mike Standish style, not knowing if it is what Lois might call a bum amount or the real deal.

He sighs, rubbing his hand along the bristle on his chin, then takes the bill, slipping it into the waistband of his pants as he steps from behind the counter. I jump back with a start, but he is only gesturing for me to follow him. We walk out the glass door and across the flyspecked parking lot, over to Room 12.

He knocks once on the mud-colored paint of the door. No sound.

He looks to me expectantly.

I knock this time. 'Lois? Are you there, Lois?'

No response.

'Look' – I turn to the man – 'she's really sick, can you–'

He pulls a passkey out of his pocket and unlocks the particleboard door.

My eyes adjust to the dark room, with its nubby curtains pulled tight across the bulging screen of the window to block out the late-afternoon light.

Mounds of sheets piled. on the bed, a faint red-brown spatter curled into one of the rivulets.

'Lois,' I blurt, unable to make it past the threshold. The clerk begins muttering loudly in Spanish.

Abruptly, amid the piles of sheets, a torn-stockinged leg surfaces. 'Whossit?'

I push past the clerk and move quickly to the bed. Lois is huddled in one corner, locks of hair matted to her face and clotted in a thin sheen of dried blood.

'Are you all right? God, Lois.'

Her dark-ridged eyelids slide open, and a sheet-creased breast slides out from under the covers.

'Alice?' She squints.

'It's Lora. Lora King,' I say. I turn to the clerk. 'Thank you.'

He pauses a long second, deciding something, probably about whether or not to call the police. Then he points a finger at me, turns, and leaves, closing the door behind him.

The room is in near darkness again, a dusty, heavy kind of late-afternoon dark. Street noises radiate in and out, carried by the hot winds.

I sit down on the edge of the bed, next to her.

'Lois, let's go. Let's get you your clothes on and I'll take you over to Alice and Bill's. Or to my place. Your pick.'

She puts a hand over her eyes and says nothing.

'We can call a doctor from there,' I add, trying desperately to see the source of the blood in the darkness.

'No doctors, sugar pie.' She rolls over and tries to prop herself up a bit.

I reach across to the bedside lamp and switch it on.

Lois rubs her eyes and manages one of her crooked smiles. A cigarette burn snarls from her collarbone.

'Oh, Lois!'

Her eyes widen a bit, then she looks down at the burn. She smiles.

'Oh, no, that's old, honey. It got infected, never healed right.'

She struggles a blue-veined, dimpled leg out from under the sheet. A garter hangs loosely atop her thigh.

'Now *that's* new.' She smirks, pointing to a long, crimson strand down the inside of her upper thigh.

'Lois,' I murmur, feeling dizzy and sick, suddenly aware of the smells of the room, the bed, a fulsome mix of bodies, drink, the slime of a lost evening and half day.

'Ah, it ain't so bad. You should have seen the other guy.' She chuckles wryly, tiredly, and gestures to the spray of dried blood. 'Busted his nose.'

'What happened?' I cover my mouth and nose with the back of my hand, unable to hold back my nausea. 'Lois, what happened?'

Her eyes light up and she is onstage, the cameras are rolling, *something*.

'The kind of dance you're lucky to make it out of, toots.' She reaches over to the bedside table and, with a growing jauntiness, pops a cigarette in her swollen lips. 'It just happens. And then happens again. But it's a walk into the lion's den. We've all got our soft spots.'

Taking a puff, she squints at me and says, 'Did you ever feel something in the dark and it gives you tingles, pinpricks under the skin, like ice on your teeth followed by a warm … a warm, velvety fist?'

I don't say anything. I feel my stomach and face go suddenly hot. I run the back of my wrist along my forehead.

Lois reaches under the sheets to pull out a silky violet dress. Throwing it over both her head and her sagging cigarette, she wriggles into its wasp waist, then turns to me.

'Honey, don't worry. I've had my insides scooped out clean after four bad turns and the clap. I've seen things and done things, had things done to me, things that…' She slides out of bed, looks down at her legs, scaled a bit on the shins with dermatitis. 'There's a lot I can get through. You, you'd best deal with your demons just the way you do now.'

I turn sharply, all the way around to face her.

'You know,' she says, through the smoke. And that is all she says. I don't know what she means, but I feel, with a shudder, that whatever she thinks she knows is probably true.

'Where are we going?'

Slouched down in the seat, Lois shifts a bit, eyes closed to the glare of passing headlights.

'La Cienega. And Manchester. With the donut on the corner.'

'Why don't you let me take you to Alice's? I think you really need to see a doctor.'

She fumbles in her ruched pocket, eyes still shut.

'Lois?'

I try again. 'Lois? Can't you let me take you to Alice's at least?'

She plucks a fresh cigarette, partly crumpled, from her pocket and punches in the car's lighter.

'I'll get taken care of where we're headed, honey. Don't worry.'

We drive in silence, listening only to the dull thud of the car over the ridges in the road. Eventually, Lois, now sucking her cigarette with vigor, turns on the radio. As the brassy music leaps out, she begins to gain energy, sitting up straight and humming along.

Finally, we approach Manchester and the ten-foot-high pink-frosted donut, sprinkles the size of baby legs.

'Turn left. It's the bungalow on the right there. The one with the chair.'

There is an orange velvet armchair on the front lawn, a magazine on its cushion, pages rippling in the evening breeze. A large radio is perched on the bungalow's porch and is billowing out what sounds like old Tin Pan Alley.

Lois is halfway out the door as I turn off the ignition. I begin to step out of the car when she swivels around and looks at me.

'Thanks, kid. Don't think I don't appreciate it.'

'Let me make sure someone's here to take care of you,' I say. As I head toward the porch, I think suddenly, as I see her there bone white and battered, that she is slipping away right in front of my eyes and that nobody will take care of her at all.

It seems to me, for no reason I can name, that if she walks up those porch steps and sets her shivery foot across the threshold, she'll sink into something even more terrifying than what I found at the motel.

187

The jabbing strains of the radio – was it 'Tiny Bubbles'? – seem to be pulling her in through sheer hypnotic force.

'I'm okay, honey.' She turns and nearly falls up the steps onto the porch. With this, the screen door gapes open with a groan, and a tall woman with a tepee of dark red curls appears. She offers a long glance at Lois.

'Oh, it's you.' Her eyebrows rise. I move a few steps closer to the porch. Lois smiles crookedly at the woman but says nothing.

'And who's that?' She gestures at me imperiously. Closer, I realize she is an older woman, maybe fifty.

'I'm a friend. I think Lois needs a doctor.'

Lois, making her way past the woman and through the doorway, looks back at me without expression.

'I'm fine,' she slurs with a brittle edge, turning back away from me and disappearing into the deep red shadows of the house.

The woman looks down at me with her hard, made-up features.

I return her gaze, unsure what to say.

She appraises me a few seconds longer, then turns, the bustle folds of her dress swinging behind her as she, too, disappears into the house. The screen door sighs back into place.

I stand there for another minute, even lean against my car and pretend to fidget for my keys. I don't know what I think might happen, but nothing does. Nothing I can see.

I settle into my car and, before leaving, jot the address down on a scrap of paper, not knowing why.

As I make the long drive home, all the women's faces along the boulevard seem to have the same look as Lois. Every one.

How can it be that, two days later, I'm in my brother's car, feeling ugly with fear, and Bill ... Bill, still numb from Edie's death and Charlie's abrupt exit, wants to talk, inexplicably, about sister-wife relations.

'Sis, I know you love Alice to death.' He turns the wheel delicately, with two fingers. 'But can you try to show it a little more?'

We are driving to our godparents' for dinner. Alice is in bed, the middle of a new round of daily migraines. It makes it easier. It lets me puzzle things out without the distractions of her sidelong gaze.

'What do you mean,' I say.

'Lately, she feels like you don't want to spend time with her. That you're distant,' he says, eyes on the road, voice soft and coaxing.

The day before, when I ran into her in the teachers' lounge, she stopped me, one spiky hand on my shoulder. 'I hear you helped

189

Lois out.'

'Yes.'

'Thanks. Thanks for that.'

Her face was as static and flat as a photograph. I felt a quiver dancing at the base of my spine.

'For what? I'm sure you would have done the same,' I replied, and as I said it I realized it was filled with meaning for her.

'Oh, yes. But she's my burden, not yours. And thanks for not telling Bill.'

In a flash, anger came over me. I wanted to say, *How dare you?*

'That's not why I didn't tell him,' I said, voice brittle. 'Not for you.'

Struck, she flashed a brilliant smile. 'I know, Lora, honey. But thanks. You're such a good sister to me.'

As I sit with Bill now, however, all I say is: 'I don't know where she gets the idea that I'm distant.'

Bill smiles faintly. 'I told her that she shouldn't have set you up so well if she didn't want to lose you to a boyfriend.'

He turns to me briefly, stopping the car at the traffic light. When he looks at me, the smile, barely perceptible, fades.

I am not smiling.

'He's not my boyfriend,' I say, gesturing to the changed light.

'Well, if he's not your boyfriend, what is he.'

He hits the gas pedal.

'Really, Lora. If he's not your boyfriend, what is he.'

It isn't a question; there is no rise at the end of the sentence.

'I see her all day at work and then on the weekends and sometimes on Wednesday nights for bridge,' I point out. 'How can you see that as neglect.'

'It's just she feels you don't confide in her like you did. Girl talk, I guess.'

'We never did that,' I say, resting my head on the heel of my hand and looking out the window. 'She's my sister-in-law.'

'Your sister, really. The most family we have.'

'I know. Okay.' It is like saying, Point taken. But it is no commitment. No commitment.

'She doesn't have many friends, and you were her friend.'

'Let's get some flowers on the way.' I point to a store.

I can't tell him – not with what I've seen, not even with this feeling of sickly dread vibrating in me.

There are things Bill can't hear. Things about her. He just can't. All I can do is find out everything I can, know everything there is to know, all she's laid her fine white hands on. It is the only way.

Looking back, I see that it was all such happenstance.

Maybe if I hadn't seen it, I would eventually have let go of the things I had seen and learned in those past few months. If I hadn't been waiting so long for Alice to show up for our ride home, I might never have picked up the newspaper's metropolitan section, sitting harmlessly on the coffee table in the teachers' lounge. And I might, so easily have missed the first article, which struck me only as very sad and somehow closer than it might have a year or two ago.

Kansas Honeymooners Find Body in Canyon
LAPD Work to ID. *Jane Doe, Dead Three Days*

(HOLLYWOOD) – A pair of newlyweds on vacation from Wichita, Kansas, were in for a grim welcome from the City of Angels Saturday when they discovered the body of a dead woman in Bronson Canyon.

Fred and Lorraine Twitchett, married less than a week ago, were on a morning stroll by the Hollywood Reservoir when they noticed what Mr. Twitchett described as 'something satiny' in the brush. Closer

192

inspection revealed it to be a torn green dress. A few yards from the dress, they came upon the corpse of a young woman wrapped in what they described as a silver shawl and naked from the waist down, except for shoes and stockings.

The woman, estimated to be between the ages of 25 and 35, was shot in the face and apparently dealt a blow to the back of the head. About five feet one and 100 pounds, the woman had dark, shoulder-length hair. Detectives will search dental records and fingerprints to determine her identity.

The corpse also had several scars of different sizes on her arms and legs that are believed to have been premortem, some weeks or more old. Several appeared to be cigarette burns, others looked to be caused by use of intravenous needles.

Police urge the public to contact them with any knowledge of a missing woman matching this general description, possibly mistreated by a husband or boyfriend, and with a possible history of narcotics use.

The next day, however, I find myself looking through the newspaper to see if there is any further information. If I hadn't seen the second article, I don't even know if I would have thought any more about it – after all, there were thousands of Hollywood girls fitting that forlorn description.

But there it is on page two.

(HOLLYWOOD) – Police have identified the Jane Doe found in Bronson Canyon just above Hollywood two days ago. A fingerprint check identified the body as that of Linda Tattersal, 27 years old, most recently of Rosecourt.

Detectives matched the victim's fingerprints through police records showing three past arrests for shoplifting, public drunkenness, and solicitation, and one conviction, last February, for resisting arrest at a roadhouse in El Segundo.

Ms. Tattersal was a member of the Screen Actors Guild from June 1953 until four months ago, when her membership was revoked for nonpayment of dues. Her last known address was at Locust Arms Apartments on Rosecourt Boulevard in Rosecourt.

'She was a nice girl,' said a neighbor in the building, who did not wish to be identified. 'But she kept bad company.'

There it is, building through paragraph one, through paragraph two, and then, my heart in my throat by the time I reach the name Locust Arms. In a flash, I see the dark tangle of pepper trees swaying out front like a warning.

I spent only ten minutes there, months

ago, and yet I suddenly can see myself walking with Alice along its cracked pavement. The door of Lois's room hanging partly open and her quavery singing voice calling us closer, beckoning us in.

Alice didn't even blink. Alice had been there many times. Alice, it struck me, had lived in dozens of places like this all her life, and for her, it was like going home.

I spread my hand over the article in the paper. I push my fingertips into the smudgy print. I wonder what I would do. I don't know anything for certain, after all.

Could Linda be Lois? Surely, Lois wasn't the only wayward girl lost in the Locust Arms, the only girl who seemed doomed to end up in Bronson Canyon or some other desolate place.

I try calling the Locust Arms, but no one will speak to me.

–Our tenants like to keep to themselves.

Or

–I don't know who you're talking about, honey.

Or

–Try Missing Persons, lady.

The next morning, I drive by the courtyard. I can't get out of the car. I stare at the row of wan doors. I wait for signs of life.

I realize I should be talking to Alice. If the girl in the paper isn't Lois, Alice could assure me that she'd just seen her friend, just got off the phone with her not the night before. Talked together confidentially just that day about the sad fate of the girl who lived across the courtyard in, say, Number 8.

That afternoon, having promised Bill, I find myself helping Alice bake cakes for the Rotary Club bake sale. As she frantically prepares three cakes for the sale and one for dessert that night, I take a seat at the kitchen table and begin peeling apples.

'Oh, Lora, I feel like we haven't talked in weeks. And first with the Beauvaises and... Well, we both get so caught up with the rest of our lives,' she says. Then, smiling, 'You with your big romance–'

She must see me bristle at the characterization because she quickly adds, '–your busy life, and we haven't made time enough lately. I want to hear everything that's been going on.'

'How's Lois?' I ask it. I ask it abruptly, like a shot to the heart.

Alice stops for just a split second, almost unnoticeably, but I see it. She stops for a hairsbreadth of a second in folding the cake batter.

'Oh, you know Lois.'

'I do,' I say, watching. Then I wait, still watching, until she has to say more. She sees I will keep waiting.

'Funny you should ask.' Alice shakes her head like a vaguely disapproving older sister. 'I guess she's gone off on another one of her tears. From what I hear, she's headed off to San Francisco without so much as a forwarding address.' Her voice, the words she chooses, seem unreal, like dialogue from a movie.

'She told you she was going to San Francisco?'

'No, not even that. A friend of hers told me. I wonder if I should put a little nutmeg in this. Do you think Bill would like that, or would it be too strong.'

'Gee, Alice, I don't know. So who told you?'

'This girl who used to work at the studio.' She puts the nutmeg back in the spice cabinet unopened. Then turns to me and smiles.

'Oh, how did you happen upon her?'

'We ran into each other at the Apple Pan.'

I look at her. Look at her and can't figure out a thing.

'With Bill,' she adds. 'We went to get a quick sandwich, and she was leaving as we were arriving.'

Just daring me to ask still more.

'What's her name?'

'I can see you're a cop's sister.' She laughs, the sound like an unbearable silver bell. 'Ina. Her name's Ina. Now do your sister-in-law a favor and hold that pan for me while I pour.'

I hold the cake pan steadily, watching her coolly, watching her watch me, wondering what I know or what I think I know. She empties the batter with great precision, twisting the bowl, shaking it just right to dispense everything evenly. Not a drop is left when she finishes. It is all very simple for her, and for every shake of my hands, hers become steadier still. I have nothing on her.

The next day, I stop by Bill's office with a surprise box of gingerbread and the excuse of needing to renew my driver's license nearby.

'So I heard you ran into an old friend of Alice's.'

He turns and looks at me.

'She told me you ran into a friend of hers.'

'She's got old friends everywhere,' Bill says, wiping his fork off with a napkin. I can see him thinking, but I'm not sure about what.

'Hmm. But this one you ran into together.'

'Yeah?'

'Ina. Her name's Ina.'

'At the Apple Pan.'

'Right. That's right. Ina,' he says. I can't read him – can't read Bill, whom I always, forever could read. But I think I detect a whiff of confusion.

'So I guess she told you that Lois Slattery

took off for San Francisco.'

'I don't know.' Bill swipes a large forkful into his mouth. 'They were talking while I was paying the bill. They went to the ladies' room together.'

'Did you know Lois had left town?'

'I don't really keep tabs on Lois Slattery,' he says, shaking his head. 'I leave that to her probation officer.'

He hooks an arm around me. 'Just between you and me, I'm kind of glad she's not around, needing Alice to take care of her all the time.'

'Was Alice giving her money?' I blurt out.

'Money? No, I don't think so. No.' He wipes his hands with his napkin.

His brow furrows ever so slightly, and my heart rises in my chest.

I struggle with the urge to put my arms around him and comfort him as I see cracks appearing all around him, spreading. He does see them spreading, doesn't he? How can he not?

Two days after seeing the second newspaper article, I determine to carry out an idea that I've formulated all night long, lying in bed, unable to sleep, hoping against all reason that Lois will call, her voice sizzling in my ear.

199

Was it all about Joe Avalon? Was he the center of this ugly story? He was in my brother's home, maybe in his bed, Edie Beauvais gone. And now, maybe Lois, too. Of course, Alice was the one everyone had in common. Everyone.

Remembering now, at parties, Alice and Edie huddled in a corner, smoking conspiratorially, giggling and flashing glances, legs swinging, rocking as they shared an ottoman, so close they were like one grinning, dangerous thing. Alice in common.

And there was mostly this: a D.A.'s investigator with a wife caught in the middle of something so lurid? However peripheral her role, it wouldn't matter. In the papers, in City Hall, it wouldn't matter. Years of hard work shot through.

As I leave my apartment that evening, I put on an old hat with a veil that hangs over my face, cobweb thick. When I arrive at the police station, I remind myself that this is not Bill's precinct, is a world away. No one will recognize me, I tell myself. Nevertheless, the dove gray veil hangs low and I try not to make eye contact with anyone as I walk into the dingy, sticky-walled station house.

I ask to speak with the detective assigned to the Linda Tattersal case, and the squinty-eyed deputy at the desk gives me a long look.

'That'd be Detective Cudahy, Miss. Can I tell him what it's about?' His finger is poised on a button on the control board.

'It's private,' I say quietly, through the veil. 'Is he in?'

The deputy looks at me again, then pushes the button, speaking into the microphone: 'Cudahy ... someone to see you.'

I sit on the adjacent bench to wait. It is several minutes before a shiny-faced man with a gritty scrub of red-blond hair walks toward me, sleeves rolled up over his red forearms. He pauses at the station desk for a moment, conferring with the deputy.

'Miss? Come with me,' he says at last, waving his arm.

He lets me pass in front of him, then guides me into a small office that smells of burnt coffee and Lysol.

He leans against the front of the desk as I sit down across from him.

'So...?' he says.

'I'm not sure... I hope I'm not wasting your time.'

'Not yet,' he says with a faint smile.

'This Linda Tattersal. From the papers. I may ... may know her.'

'But you're not sure,' he says, pushing the door shut with his outstretched leg.

'I know a woman named Lois who lived in Rosecourt.'

'That so?'

'At the Locust Arms.'

'I see,' he says, arms folded across his chest. 'You always wear a veil like that in this heat?'

I feel my face turn warm. I try to lift the veil, catching it on my eyelashes.

'Let me help,' he says, reaching out and pushing the veil up. My hand wavers.

'So you know a Lois in Rosecourt, huh?'

'I do. I mean, she did live there, at those apartments. And she fits the physical description.'

'She's a friend of yours.'

I pause, looking at him. 'Listen. All I'm suggesting is that I think it may be her. They may be the same person.'

'How do you know this Lois?'

'I'm sorry, I...' I tug at my skirt. 'I guess I don't see how that matters. Don't you want to find out if it's the same girl?'

'Why? Did Someone want to hurt your friend?' He cocks his head.

'I just ... if it's Lois, *my* Lois, she ... she had scars.'

'Lots of people have scars, Miss ... I'm sorry, what's your name?'

'Okay, she'd have *specific* scars. She'd have lots of them. On her arms. Needle marks.'

'That was in the papers, yeah.'

I twist in my seat. 'She'd also have them other places.'

'Yeah?'

'She'd have them all kinds of places. Behind her knees. Between her toes. On her neck.' I find myself pointing two fingers to my own neck.

'She'd have them everywhere,' I finish.

His arms drop a little.

'And she'd have a cigarette burn, right here.' I touch my collarbone lightly.

'And dermatitis on her legs. Maybe old burns on her thighs from a fire.'

His arms fall, and he reaches out for a pad of paper and pen.

'And she'd have scar tissue from ... from several abortions.' This is little more than a guess but a confident one (*'I've had my insides scooped out clean after four bad turns...'*)

He meets my eyes.

'Okay, Miss, we'd better start here,' he says as he grabs the phone, barking into the receiver, 'Get me the morgue.'

And it's this. It's this:

Could that thing there, that block of graying flesh, be Lois? Could it be a woman at all? The morgue attendant picks pieces of dust and gravel from the place her face had been. He's trying to get a footprint.

'I think after he does her, he kicks her over on her face with his foot,' the attendant says.

He says this to Detective Cudahy.

I'm standing in the corner.

'I didn't know you were working on her

right now,' says Cudahy. He looks at me.

From the side, from where I've backed up, nearly to the far wall, it looks like she has a big flower in her hair, like Dorothy Lamour. A big blossom, dark and blooming.

If I don't focus, don't squint, I can pretend it's a flower and not a hole, a gaping cavity.

'It's going to be hard to tell,' he says. 'But try your best.'

He reaches his hand out, summoning me over with lowered eyes.

'She was a mess even before,' the attendant notes, tilting his head. 'Her skin...'

I touch my fingertips to my mouth as I walk over. I wonder if there's any way at all that I will be able to look long enough to tell.

'There's no...' What I want to say is that there's no face there. There's nothing there at all. But I can't quite get the words out. Instead, I just stare down into the shiny, blackened pit before me.

'You want to focus on the rest of her,' Cudahy says quietly. 'Body size, shape. The places you remember scars.'

I look at the stippled body, I look at its pocks and wounds. I look – knowing this will be it for me – at the hands. Lois's stubby little hands, her doll fingers with her strangely square fingertips. They're there, right in front of me. They're little doll hands, and they're covered with ink, torn at the tips in places, ragged and stringy at the edges but definitely hers. They're Lois's hands.

I teeter back slightly on my heels. Cudahy's hand is pressed on my back, holding me up. My head swims and then I see the welts on her breasts and below her belly. I see them and I remember the Rest E-Z Motel. I remember everything.

'So it's her, huh?' A voice sounds out.

'It's her,' another voice answers.

It's my own.

'We'll need to start at the top,' Detective Cudahy says, uncapping his pen and smoothing a rough hand over a pad of lined paper.

'Right.'

'What's your full name?'

This is when I realize the extent of what I have done. And this is when I find myself not knowing why I feel the need to lie. But I do feel I need to lie.

'Susan. Willa. Morgan,' I say slowly, pulling each part from my class roster. Susan Wiggins, Willa Johnston, and Eleanor Morgan will never know the dark tunnels into which their names have been thrown.

'Age?'

'Twenty-eight.'

'Married?'

'No.'

'How did you know the victim?'

'She used to come into a nightclub I go to sometimes.' I am on eerie autopilot, unsure from where I am getting the words coming out of my mouth. My voice even sounds different: vaguely brittle and with a slight lilt.

'What nightclub?'

'The Red Room Lounge.'

'In Rosecourt?'

'No, Hollywood. It's on Hollywood Boulevard.'

'She told you her name was Lois?'

'Yes.'

'Last name?'

'She never said.' I don't know why I lie about this. I'm going solely by instinct. Somehow I want him to think I didn't know her well, not well at all. *If I knew her well enough to know her last name, wouldn't I have known enough to stop—*

'What was she doing there?'

'Passing the time,' I say with a shrug.

'Is that what you were doing there?' he asks, scribbling, not meeting my gaze.

I straighten in my seat. 'I would go with my girlfriends. Sometimes on a date.'

'What kinds of dates?' He looks up at me with a slight pause.

'Kinds of dates? What do you mean?'

He looks at me for a moment. 'Skip it,' he says, returning to his writing pad. 'How regular would you see her there?'

'Once or twice a month.'

'How'd you happen to talk with her?'

'I don't know. I think maybe someone I was with knew her or vice versa. I really can't remember.'

'What kinds of things did you talk about?' He continues writing.

'Girl stuff. Hair, men.' I try a smile. 'She was doing some acting and modeling.'

'Modeling?'

'That's what she said.'

'What do you do?'

'Pardon? What?'

'Do you have a job?'

'Yes, I ... I give sewing lessons.' I don't know where this comes from.

He writes something down. Then, 'Did she ever tell you about any men she dated? Men she knew?'

'Yes.' Here is my chance. 'She told me once about a man who would ... do things to her.'

'Things?'

'She would have burn marks. He would burn her.'

'With cigarettes?'

'Yes.'

'Did they use narcotics together?'

'I don't know.'

'But you knew she used them.'

'I saw the marks.'

'And you knew what they meant?'

'I don't use narcotics, Detective, if that's what you mean.'

'Was she very scared of this guy?'

'I guess. She must have been. But she'd been, you know, around the block a few times. Nothing much surprised her.'

'Did she tell you anything about this man? What he did? Where he lived?'

'He worked in the movies,' I say, tightening my fingers over my purse. 'He worked for a studio.'

'Which studio?'

'I don't know. She worked for RKO and Republic. I do know that.'

'So you think he did, too? Did you get the idea he might have got her jobs?'

'I don't know.'

'Did she tell you anything else about him?'

'No.'

'When was the last time you saw her?'

'A few weeks ago.' Here, because it seems easier, safer, I just lie. Somehow telling him about the recent episode at the Rest E-Z Motel seems too risky, too involved.

'At the Red Room Lounge?'

'Yes. Right. The Red Room.'

He pushes a piece of paper over at me.

'I want all your information and any names you can remember of anyone you ever saw her with. Don't forget your phone number and address.'

I stare at the paper for a second. Then, I

take the pen and begin writing.

'So.' He leans back, stretching his arms a bit as I write. 'How do you think she ended up in water?'

I look up with a start.

'Water?'

'So you don't know everything, Miss Morgan?' I feel my hand shake around the pen.

'I don't know anything. What water?'

'You tell me. Your friend drowned.'

My head is throbbing when Detective Cudahy hands me the glass of warmish water. I can't keep my lies straight. I slide my hat off my head and into the palm of my hand. It is moist where my forehead has strained against it.

'You're telling me she didn't die from being ... from being shot.' Unconsciously, I touch my hand to my own face.

'The shot was postmortem.'

'So it was all an accident? She just drowned?'

'I don't think so. Accidental drowning victims don't usually end up with their faces blown off.'

'Why was she shot then?'

He tilts his head. 'Could be to try and prevent identification of the body. Or he's just in a violent rage. It's hard to tell just yet. She wasn't in the water that long. Just long enough to fill her lungs and sink her like a stone.'

I twitch, involuntarily. 'But the papers...'

'She was found in the Hills, but we kept the water stuff out of the press. It may help down the line.'

'So she drowned and then someone shot her and then just ... just dumped her there?'

'Far as we can tell.'

'Drowned in the ocean?'

'Salt water.'

'What would Lois have been doing in the ocean?'

'Thought maybe you could tell me. Her boyfriend have a boat?'

'I don't ... know,' I say, trying to process it all. Trying not to think of Lois, face in dark water, floating.

'Maybe you'll ask around for us.' He looks at me hard in the eyes. 'In your circles, you might be able to find out things we can't.'

At this, I almost want to laugh.

'I'll try. I will,' I reply, not knowing what I mean by it.

You have to ask it: Who would cry for Lois Slattery, with all her slurry glamour, her torn and fast-fading beauty – beauty mostly because you could see it vanishing before your eyes? Her loss meant nothing and she would not be missed, not even by me. I wouldn't miss her – not in a way as true as she deserved.

But there was something that lingered, her whole life a dark stain, spreading. A pulsing energy racked tight and always threatening to burst through its borders, its hems, its ragged, straining edges. She would have been happy to know how ripely powerful she would become in death. She had been waiting for it.

The next day ... the next day, very early, I am walking from the office to my classroom. I'm thinking of how many days it's been since I've seen Mike Standish, how many calls of his I've left unreturned. He is filled with the promise of distraction. But now is not a time for distraction.

I'm walking through the still-empty hallways when I feel her. I feel her even before I see her, hear her. She's leaning against the door of my classroom, humming and patting her nose with a powder puff from the ivory compact in her hand.

'So our carpool days are over,' she says evenly, looking only in the mirror.

'I have a lot of new responsibilities,' I say, walking closer.

'I understand,' she says, snapping the compact shut and looking at me.

I try so hard to read her, to read the look in her eyes. I try so hard I feel I'll bore through.

But she just smiles impersonally, superbly, like a showroom model, a beauty queen.

'Well, let's not forget, Lora.'

'Forget what?'

'About us. Sisters,' she says. 'About how we're sisters.'

Alice pulls open my classroom door for me. A draft whistles through from within.

'Who could forget?' I say, hard. 'Who could forget that?'

She only smiles in return, and in her smile I can see nothing, not a stray flicker of fear or anger or anything at all. But what I now know is this: There's a reason she's wearing this blankness, this mechanical look stripped of her heat, energy, her intermittent chaos. There's a reason she's wearing this face. And I'm the reason.

Ellie Marbury, fifteen years old with gum in the corner of her mouth, wearing a sloppy joe sweater the vague color of store-bought pound cake, is whispering feverishly to Celeste Dutton as I try to keep the attention of twenty girls on a warm Friday afternoon.

When I confront both girls after class, Ellie, with all the petulance of a teenager unaware she is already at the height of her rather wan beauty and it will all be downhill from here, asserts, 'Mrs. King sure was acting funny today.'

'Oh?' I say, emptily.

Ellie's eyes grow wide. 'Y-e-a-h,' she says, stretching the word out and spitting her gum into the trash can I hold before her.

'She kept running over to the window and running all around the room.'

'It was like she had ants in her pants or something.' Celeste, always acting younger than her age, giggles.

'And then she told everyone that one day we'd understand how hard it is to be a woman,' Ellie adds, half snickering and half eyes popping. Both girls seem torn between laughter and discomfort.

'She said wait until they come sniffing around you,' Celeste burbles. 'And Ellie said who, and Mrs. King said be glad you still have to ask.'

'And she meant *men*,' Ellie nods. 'I *knew*. We *all* did. I just wanted to see if she would say it.'

And then I realize, abruptly, that Ellie, for all her bravado, all her eye-rolling teenage sarcasm, is about to cry. Despite the bubble gum pink smirk on her face, I can see tears are itching to pop from the corners of her powder blue eyes.

I know I should put my hand under her

chin and reassure her somehow. But I don't.

'And then ... and then...' Ellie's face is just seconds, mere seconds from bursting. 'She said that once they find the dark holes be-be-be-between our legs, no matter how good it is, everything turns to s-s-s-s-shit. Excuse me, Miss King, but that is what she said.'

Celeste's eyes grow wide with pleasure at her friend's daring, but I know better. I put my hand sharply on Ellie's shoulder and direct her out of the room.

She's just made it into the hallway, the classroom door has just slammed shut behind us, when glassy tears tear open her once-smug face. Somehow Ellie has understood something about what she has seen, about what Alice has shown her. Why she understands, I don't want to know.

'It's okay, Ellie,' I say, leaning against the lockers. 'You're not in trouble.'

'Thanks, Miss King,' she says, tears jetting unabated. 'I know I'm not.'

She rubs the long sleeve of her sweater over her face. 'Don't tell, okay?'

Then she pulls her old face together, tight and contemptuous. 'Don't tell.'

And I won't. It would be one too many private dramas, after all.

It is late, after nine, after a long student assembly, and my head is still ringing from the sounds of throngs of teenage girls straining gracelessly to mimic Kay Starr.

I make my way quickly through the noiseless lot, where only a handful of cars remain.

As I near my car, a dark sedan lights up suddenly and veers over toward me. I scramble for my keys, guessing it is only a colleague wanting to share a commiserating good night but not wanting to take any chances.

As I slide into my front seat, the car pulls up beside me.

'So ... this is where you work. I wouldn't have guessed girls who moved in your circles taught school.'

I turn my head, recognizing the familiar voice.

'Hello, Detective,' I murmur.

Cudahy faces me with a grim-eyed stare. 'Get in,' he orders, reaching across and opening his passenger side door.

I do as he says, trying not to meet his eyes.

'Isn't this out of your jurisdiction?' I bluff.

'Yes,' he says.

'I had you pegged for a liar, but not that

kind of liar,' Cudahy says.

I feel my face burn and wonder what he knows, other than that I am obviously not the kind of girl who is a regular at places like the Red Room Lounge.

'You don't understand.'

'Sure I do, Miss Morgan. You figure, What's the harm? What's a dumb cop going to know? I'll have a little fun with him. Get my kicks.'

'No. No. I wanted to help, but I had these ... responsibilities.'

'Who to?'

'No, you've got me really wrong here. Horribly wrong.'

'You just protecting yourself or someone else too?'

'I've got nothing to do with it,' I say, still not looking at him directly. 'I know Lois through someone else. Lois is a friend of someone ... close to me. Lois *was* a friend of someone close to me.'

'Don't you think it's about time you started spilling it? Honest, I'm three seconds away from booking you. You've hampered a police investigation, lied to authorities–'

'Please. I do know Lois. I told you: I know she used narcotics. I know she was selling herself.' I pause, deciding whether I should hazard a guess about Joe Avalon's role. 'And I know that she had a ... someone who arranged things.'

'And who'd that be?'

I can't think fast enough. All I can think of is my face, blazing with shame. 'Don't you already know? I can't be the only person you've found who knew that.'

He looks at me long and hard, rubbing his chin and glaring. 'I don't know what you're doing to me here. I don't know– Look, I'm a real sap not to just bring you in. I'm doing you a big favor, but only if you can give me something.'

'He lives in Bunker Hill. You must know who he is. He takes care of everything for RKO, maybe others.'

I feel the weight of the gaze from the corners of my eyes.

'I don't know...' A horrible pressure on my chest.

He reaches into his glove compartment and pulls out a folder, tossing it over to me. I open it with shaking fingers.

It is a photo of a man I've never seen before, with a lanky mustache and yellow eyes.

'I don't know who this is,' I say, relieved. I start to hand it back to him when the photo slips and another appears behind it.

There he is.

Droopy eyes, bushy black brows and lashes. I turn the photo over and see, in small type, 'Joseph Nathanson alias Johnny Davalos alias Joe Avalon 06/25/12.'

'Okay,' Cudahy say. 'Okay, then. Lucky guess.'

I look up at him. 'I don't know anything specific. I just figured...'

'So who's this person who introduced you to Lois Slattery? Davalos?'

'No, no.'

I feel my throat go dry. A voice, some voice, rises up from inside. 'You won't involve me at all?'

He sighs and looks down at the photo hard. 'I can't promise I won't need to contact you. But I won't push you.'

I breathe in fast.

'Edith Ann Beauvais.' It is a chance. I take a chance.

He writes the name down. 'Who's she?'

'She was someone who... I saw her with them a few times.'

'Davalos and the victim?'

'Yes.' I am losing track of my own distortions.

'Where does she live?'

'She's dead.'

'Convenient.'

'She killed herself.'

'We'll see how what you say checks out. Does she have any surviving relatives?'

'I guess. I mean, her husband.'

'Name?'

'Charlie Beauvais.'

'Where might I find him?'

'He's gone.'

'He's gone. Of course. Where'd he go? Hop a ship to the Orient?'

'No one's sure. Maybe Mexico.'

'What are you doing to me?'

'Telling you the truth.'

He sighs again, looks out the window for a minute, then turns back to me.

'Don't you want to ask me something?'

I look at him.

'Don't you want to know how I found you?'

I swallow hard, although I'm not sure why. 'How did you find me?'

'Police business.'

'Oh.'

'But you might think about this: I found *you* by accident. Because I was following someone else. Imagine my surprise. You get it?'

'I'm not sure.'

He gestures with his eyes to the Avalon photo. 'Watch your back, Miss.'

Like out of a movie. Like out of a movie, and I clutch my chest. I clutch my chest and shake my head. I didn't see it coming, but I should have.

The next day at school, I keep worrying about when I will see Alice for the first time, for the first time since this most recent conversation with Detective Cudahy. These days she seems to be lurking around every corner.

As I make my way down the stairs after fifth period, I am surprised instead to see my brother standing in the front vestibule, kicking his foot in short strokes against the blasted brick of the wall. My *brother*, I almost say it aloud.

He must have heard my approach, or somehow sensed me descending, because he immediately turns to see me.

His face has a pinched, anxious look I know very well. It is the face he wears when he feels helpless. Seeing it, I stop short. I can't bear to move closer.

'What's wrong, Bill?'

'Nothing's wrong, nothing. Why do you ask?'

I am still a few steps from the bottom, but somehow I can't get any closer. Why is he here? Has something happened? Has he found something out?

I can't say anything. It is long past saying anything.

He runs the back of his hand over his face. 'It's nothing. It's nothing. It's just– When you drove Alice to school today, did she seem all right to you?'

I make the words come out. 'I didn't drive her today. I had an early meeting. I've had a lot of early meetings lately.'

He turns toward the wall, touching it with his fingertips. Suddenly, he is nine years old again and facing the profuse tears of his sister, who doesn't want to leave for girls' camp the next day.

'What is it, Bill?'

'And she's not here. She hasn't been here all day. They said she called in sick. They called me at work to see if I could pick up her students' assignments and take them home. They…' He trails off.

'She's probably at home in bed. A mis-understanding–'

'Yes.' He lifts his head. 'I'm sure. Obvious. Thanks, Sis. You know me, overreacting as usual.'

I try for a smile and walk the final steps, moving toward him.

'She's just been a little sick, so I've tried to keep a close eye on her.'

'Yes, of course. I'm sure she appreciates it.' Then I add, touching his arm lightly, 'It's what you do.'

He turns his head and looks at me, his eyes fastening on mine, *my eyes*. 'That's right, Sis.

You always know. You always knew.'

After he leaves, I shut the door to my classroom and lock it. I sit at my desk for ten minutes, ignoring the students gathering in the hallway. I don't even hear their rising clatter. I sit at my desk, hands folded, looking out the window, thinking, knowing things. Things I will have to do.

He wouldn't tell me. He'd just make it go away.

I haven't seen him in ten long days, since before seeing Lois's body. Have been avoiding him, not wanting to feel tempted to tell him about Lois, afraid, in part maybe, that he might already know. I haven't returned the calls he's left with the front desk of my apartment building. I don't let myself think about it. If I start to think about it, I remind myself who introduced us.

At night, when I'm trying to sleep, pictures of them together gather in my head. Mike and Alice in the far corner of the room, her head thrown back in laughter as he talks in her ear. Mike and Alice smoking on the back porch at one of her parties, each making droll faces, telling old jokes. Who knows how many conversations? Who could guess all that had passed from his wry mouth to her tilted ear? Then from her mouth to... anywhere. There is something so horrible in the thought of that, so horrible that I shut it all down. I shut it all down until I feel nothing.

And then there he is.

Standing in the hallway in front of the door to my apartment. His hat is pushed back, and he is fishing through his coat pocket.

He looks up and sees me, eyes dancing. 'So what, you're finished with me, is that it?' But smiling, always smiling.

I don't say anything. I reach into my purse to retrieve my key.

'Kind of a shabby way to let me know. Hearing from the building manager that I'm no longer allowed in when you're not here.'

Leaning his shoulder against the wall, he pulls out a cigarette and lights it.

It is true. Two days before, I told the manager not to let him or anyone else in. After what Detective Cudahy said, I couldn't take any chances.

I unlock the door and walk in, leaving it open for him to follow.

I turn on a lamp, and he sets his hat down on a table.

'Why would you want to be here when I'm not here?' I say as I walk around the back of the sofa and flip on two more lights.

He sits down and returns to his cigarette. 'To wait for you. Like you do at my place. Or like you used to do.'

I sit down on the arm of the chair across from him, folding my hands in my lap.

'And now you don't even offer me a drink.' He throws his hands in the air and shakes his head. 'That's how it is, is it? I gotta tell you, King, this is not something that happens to me all the time.'

'Not with someone like me, you mean.'

He meets my gaze and talks through the cigarette. 'That's right. That's exactly right.'

'If you wanted to get in my apartment so badly, what stopped you? Don't all you press agents have ways to get in places you're not supposed to be?'

'I didn't know it was a place I wasn't supposed to be,' he says, blowing a gust of smoke at me. 'I guess if I had, I would have brought my set of pick locks and just– You think I'm a real snake, don't you? Jesus, Lora, how could you have sullied yourself so long with me?'

He is good. His face displays genuine injury. Of course, I remind myself, putting on a first-class front is his bread and butter.

'Why would you want to be here when I'm not?' I say again, my mind continually rotating back to his connection with Alice, his history with Alice.

He twists his head from side to side with irritation. 'I told you, King. I came to see you. You weren't here. I was going to wait. Scandalous.'

'Why would you think I would be here? Did you call first?'

'I guess I didn't give it all that much thought,' he says, with more than a little annoyed sarcasm. 'Call me irresponsible.'

'What did you think you might find?'

'Find?' His eyebrows lift.

'I'm not as naïve as you think.'

'Jesus.' He punches out his cigarette. 'Okay. If that's how you want to play it. If I wanted to come when you weren't here, why would I be waiting for you?'

'How do I know you were waiting for me?'

'This could go on forever. I don't know what dark secrets you think your apartment holds for me, but to tell you the truth, I'm not that interested. Maybe it's me who should be asking you questions. Why don't you just tell me who the guy is?'

'What guy?' I say.

'The one you're tossing me for. I hear he's a badge.'

'A badge.'

'A cop, or a police detective. Which makes for a kind of poetic justice.' He pushes out a faint wrinkle in his gabardines and leans back, folding his arms behind his head.

'Poetic? ... I don't...' Has he seen me with

Detective Cudahy?

'What, did you think Alice wouldn't tell me?'

I feel a cold blast across my chest. She is always so many steps ahead.

'Alice...' My mind reels. I slide down off the arm onto the chair cushion. How much could she know about Detective Cudahy? I realize suddenly that whatever she has figured out, or guessed at, she is determined to make sure that I know about it. Know she is watching.

'So when did you decide you preferred hot dog stands and chop suey joints to Ciro's and Mocambo?' Mike continues.

Alice. I try to pull myself together. I close my eyes, place a hand on either side of my head, and try to focus. *Don't think about it now, don't think about it now, just find out how, why, anything you can.*

'What are you so upset about, King?' I hear him get up and move over to the bar cart. 'I'm the one who got played.'

He pours me a short drink and walks it over to me before getting one for himself.

I gulp it and look up at him.

'Who's being played?' My voice sounds funny. 'For God's sake. Are you just some kind of spy? A snitch? Did she tell you to take me out, *seduce me* just so she can keep tabs on me?' It doesn't sound like me. It sounds fast, hard and crackling, my teeth chattering with nerves.

'Seduce you?' He chortles. 'King, is that really how you remember it?'

'What, do you tell her everything about me, about us?'

He stops laughing and throws me a severe look I've never seen on him. 'That's right. I tell her ev-erything. Let's see.' He looks up, as though trying to recollect and begins counting off on his fingers. 'I told her how I had you in my bed within three hours of meeting you. I told her how you'd come by my place for a late-night fuck after you'd been on dates with other men. I told her how you liked to be flipped in bed and how you like it when I push your face into the pillow. I told her how–'

'You're a real bastard.'

'King.' He shakes his head. 'I didn't tell her a thing. I don't know where you got the idea that I'm such a cad. The worst you could say about me is I don't mind keeping secrets. Including yours.'

'I'm sorry,' I say, because suddenly, forcefully I believe him. Something raw in his eyes amid all the polish and flash. Something I've never seen before.

'Now,' he says, reaching for the bottle he'd set on the coffee table and pouring us both another drink. 'Isn't it time you told me what's going on?'

I pause for a moment, but there he is,

there he is. And I do it. I tell him what I know about Alice and Lois, and then I tell him about going to get Lois at the Rest E-Z Motel. And then I tell him about Edie Beauvais and Joe Avalon, and about seeing the articles in the paper and, last, about seeing Lois's body in the morgue. I tell him many things, but not everything. Without thinking, I instinctively leave out anything about what I have done and said to keep Bill's name as far out of it as possible.

Mike listens to it all, smoking a new cigarette and not speaking. When I finish, he leans forward, squinting through the billow in front of him.

'Is that everything?'

'Isn't that enough?'

'There are some things I can help you with. Some things I can tell you.'

'I thought maybe.'

'So why didn't you talk to me before?'

'I didn't trust you.' There is no kind way to say it. And I am through with being kind.

He looks at me. 'But you do now?'

'I'm not sure how much of it is trust and how much is desperation,' I say, truthfully.

'Nobody ever is,' he says, stubbing out his cigarette. 'Joe Avalon, that fellow, he hustles women for people in the business. I guess you figured that out. I've seen him before. In my line, he's one of the numbers you call. Some of these guys can be counted on more than others. Some end up in the blackmail business.'

'Is he one of them?'

'Maybe. I don't know. Sure, I wouldn't put it past him. But I can't be positive.'

'Did you know he knew Lois?'

'No.'

'What else do you know about him?'

'He worked for Walter Schor a lot.'

'I know.' I tell him about seeing Joe Avalon coming from meeting a Mr. Schor at the studio. 'Who is Schor exactly?'

'A big gun. Very high up at the studio. Avalon must be doing well for himself. He gets to skip the go-betweens. Like me,' he adds. 'But you can't be surprised by any of this.'

'No. Is that all you can tell me? Do you think Lois worked for Joe Avalon?'

Mike rubs his eyes and pauses. Then, 'Of course.'

'Do you think Alice worked for Joe Avalon?'

He pauses again, eyeing me. 'Of course.'

I feel my torso lift suddenly, as if in shock, but I am too numb to feel shock. 'Why...'

'How else would she know a guy like that? Even if she also bought drugs from him, I'd be surprised if she hadn't worked for him at one time.'

'Bought drugs?'

'He sells dope, too. They all do. Or at least

he's a middleman. Don't you think he's the one who was so good at keeping Lois half bent?'

'I see,' I say. 'And Alice?'

'Alice used to take bennies – Benzedrine – when she worked at the studio. All kinds of pep pills. A lot of them do. I don't know if she still does.'

I think about Alice, about her manic hostessing, her frenzied housework, her rabid energy, and her occasionally surging speech. And I think about her days in bed with 'migraines,' her disappearances from school, the thin enamel of sweat that often gleamed off her body.

'And what did Alice do for him?'

'What do you think?' He rakes a hand through his immaculate hair. 'She found girls. She found all the girls, Lora. I saw her do it. She knew them all, the Girl with the Tape. She met them that way. Word was she'd pick out the ones she thought would sell. Is that what you want?'

An image flashes before my eyes: Alice on her knees, pins in her mouth, measuring Lois for her Indian Girl costume. I swallow hard and push forward. 'What else?'

'Let's stop here for now.' He straightens his tie and jacket. 'I'll tell you a few more things on the way.'

'On the way?'

'We're going to the studio.'

'Why?'

'It may not be as exciting as tailing people, but old-fashioned bureaucratic files can do a lot of talking.'

As we drive, my mind swirling, Mike talks.

'She'd call me and want to meet for lunch, and then she'd ask me if we'd slept together and what it was like, what I did and what you did. Did you know that?'

'What did you say?'

'I generally don't kiss and tell, but that rule doesn't usually apply to telling women, or women like Alice. But somehow I couldn't tell her. Somehow ... I just didn't,' he says, then laughs. 'Maybe some kind of press agent instinct.'

'What did she want to know?'

'Everything. And she'd want to know if you would feel bad about what you'd done. And she'd want to know if you ever liked it to hurt, liked it rough, you know?'

'What did you tell her?'

He looks over at me with his lazy smile. 'I lied. But I don't think she believed me.'

'No,' I say, feeling my face turn hot. 'I guess I wouldn't either.'

He grabs my hand lightly, fingertips touching my palm. It is so genuine a gesture that it startles me. I resist both the urge to pull my hand away and the urge to seize his tightly.

'D-d-does' – my mouth inexplicably

tripping me up – 'does my brother know about you and Alice? Your history?'

'Oh, God, no. I'm sure he doesn't. She is nothing if not careful about what your brother knows.'

'I suppose that's right.'

The warren of offices has an eerie silver chill at night. The sound of our shoes seems unbearably loud. Even though I know Mike is allowed to be here – this is his work, after all – I can't get past the feeling we are trespassing. I speak barely above a hush.

'You don't need to whisper yet.' Mike smirks. 'We're still in legit territory.'

We pass through several winding corridors without seeing a soul.

'Some people are around, but not in this building. They'd be over on the soundstages – or else the writers in their building across the street. I doubt we'll see anyone.'

I follow Mike into a suite of offices. SECURITY is etched in glass on the first door. We move through an outer office and up to a door marked WARREN DIXON, CHIEF OF SECURITY.

Mike reaches into his pocket and pulls out a sterling key ring.

'You have a key to his office?'

He smiles again. 'It's my job, King. When that barrel-chested all-American box office champ gets caught pants around his ankles in the back room of Café Zombie, sharing a needle with a twelve-year-old hustler, I need to be able to fix it fast.'

He unlocks the office door and pushes it open before me. 'And this is the place to start.'

I walk in, my feet sinking into carpet as thick as a sponge. 'Here?'

He breezes past me and moves to the other side of the dim office, illuminated by large set lights across the street. As I follow, he raps his fingers on a paneled door. 'Files. Secrets enough to bury an industry.'

'You don't have to impress me,' I say. 'And if you're allowed in here, why can't we turn on the lights?'

'No need to draw extra attention.' He grins, opening the door.

I was expecting a closet, but it is a large windowless room, twice as big as the office that led into it, filled with filing cabinets with mahogany fronts.

Before my eyes can adjust to the bright lights, Mike is opening a long drawer marked 'Personnel – Costume – 1950-52.'

'I think she moved here from Universal in 'fifty-one,' he says, his fingers dancing along the colored tabs.

'And there she is.' He whistles, pulling out what strikes me as a disproportionately large folder marked 'Steele, Alice.'

As if reading my mind, Mike says, 'She

worked here for, what, just two years and her file is bigger than Joan Crawford's.'

'May I see?' I say, tiptoeing over his arm.

'Yeah, yeah,' he mutters, paging through furiously. 'Just let me pull out the relevant stuff. There's a lot of administrative material we don't want to waste our time with.'

'Maybe I should decide that,' I say.

He stops for a second and looks at me, raising an eyebrow. 'Still don't trust me, eh?'

'I trust you enough,' I say. 'Enough for some things.'

'Well, fasten your eyes on this.' He hands me a document bearing the black stamp PERSONAL AND CONFIDENTIAL. 'If I got caught showing you this, I'd be on a plane back to Connecticut. That's trust, King.'

It holds a copy of a police report. Alice P. Steele, *9/14/52*. Suspect was arrested outside the Black Flamingo nightclub. Pandering. Solicitation. Public drunkenness. Suspected narcotics use. Assaulting an officer.

'But she was never formally charged? She'd have been fired.'

'She must have had friends in high places. Friends within these walls. We may take care of the talent, but costume girls don't normally rate such treatment.'

'Joe Avalon and his ... clients?'

'You got it.' He pulls out another document. 'Didn't you say Alice graduated from someplace in Van Nuys?'

I remember my conversation with Principal Evans. 'Well, that's what she said.'

'According to her personnel papers, she never graduated high school.'

'I guess I knew that was a lie,' I say.

'A reprimand.'

'Pardon?'

'This memo shows that her bosses in Costume reprimanded her for what they call 'improper conduct and questionable behavior.' I'd have to talk to Costume to find out what that was about. Could be anything from tardiness to giving head to the grips–' He stops himself and smiles at me. 'Pardon me.'

I pull out a cache of paper from behind the memo. Paging through, I can't find anything relating to Joe Avalon/John Davalos, Walter Schor, or Lois Slattery.

'Would Lois have a file?'

Mike returns Alice's to the drawer and walks over to a set of cabinets entitled 'Extras.'

'No...' he says, shuffling through the folders.

'Try Linda Tattersal.'

'Bingo.'

The folder is slim. It has only a carbon copy of basic personnel information.

'The police probably took the rest,' I realize.

Mike looks at me briefly, then looks back

down at the form. 'Not much here.'

I look at the form.

'Five five one seven oh six Manchester.'

'What?'

The address strikes me suddenly. Lois lived so transiently that I didn't expect it to have any significance, but it does.

'Where is that?'

'Hell if I know.' Mike shrugs. 'Not my part of town.'

'Could that be Manchester and La Cienega?'

'I don't know, why?' His eyes look strangely bright, his hand on the folder I'm still holding.

'Just wondering,' I say. I look at the name listed next to the address, the spot usually reserved for landlords or landladies. It reads, 'Olive MacMurray.'

'What are you looking at?' Mike asks, placing his other hand on my shoulder.

'Nothing,' I say. I wonder if she is the woman I saw when I dropped Lois off at the house on Manchester after picking her up at the Rest E-Z Motel.

But somehow I don't want to tell Mike that. The more he asks, the less inclined I feel to tell. He seems too eager to leave, to wrap things up.

He takes the folder from my hands.

'Sorry this wasn't more help,' he says, opening the drawer and slipping the folder back in its place.

'That's okay.'

'Let's go grab a nightcap, King. Sit on this a little.'

'I'm tired. Maybe we'd just better call it a night.'

The next day, I leave work early and drive the same route I had with Lois, along La Cienega, all the way to the large display donut, its slightly rusting candy sprinkles nearly shaking from it.

At the door, I take a deep breath and ring the shrill, over-sprung bell.

It is the same tall woman with the crimson cone of curls on top of her head, her brows pinch-knitted red on her forehead. She appraises me with cool suspicion through the screen door.

'Miss MacMurray?'

Squinting, a cigarette wedged in her scarlet-edged lips, she mutters, 'It's Mrs. What do you want?'

'I wondered if I might have a moment of your time.'

She surveys me, from the pale, custard-colored hat on my head to my pigskin pumps.

'No God stuff here,' she finally says,

starting to shut the door.

There doesn't seem to be any way to get into that house much less get the information I want. In the basted pocket of my dress, I grasp my only bargaining chip.

'Oh,' I say, waving my hand. 'I'm not one of those. I just have some questions for you.'

'That's how it always starts.'

'It's about Lois Slattery,' I blurt out, just as the closing door nearly blocks my view of her.

She pulls the door back with a jerk, raising an eyebrow in a way that looks painful, like risking the opening of a wound.

'Don't know who you're talking about.'

'But you do.' I try to fix a stare.

She pauses, then says, with a faint snarl, 'Who are you to me, anyway? I don't talk at all and I don't talk to just anybody.'

'I'm an acquaintance of Joe Avalon.'

She smirks so bodily that the powder on her chalky bosom rises, hangs in the air for a minute, and then falls again.

'I don't think so, honey, but that's just funny enough to get you inside.'

She props open the door with one acid green slipper. I hurry past it and into the darkened living room.

'Twenty and I'll listen,' she says, sitting down on a worn velvet armchair much like the one on the front lawn.

I can barely see in the dim space, but what

I can discern seems strangely unlived in. A sofa that matches the armchair, a large radio of the kind common before the war, a fringed lamp wrapped in dust. Otherwise, the room is bare.

Through an open door I can see a bedroom empty save a bed with a bare mattress on top and a pile of towels at the foot.

Nobody lives here. They pass through.

'Twenty,' she repeats.

'Pardon?' I sit down on the low edge of the sagging sofa, my knees nearly reaching my chin. 'Oh, of course.'

I reach into my purse and hand Mrs. MacMurray a bill, hoping that money won't be her sole bartering interest. If so, the meeting will be over soon after it starts.

'You don't know Joe Avalon,' she says, sliding the bill into the pocket of her robe and folding her maroon-lipped talons in her lap.

'I do.'

'How?'

'That's not important.'

'I'll be the judge of that,' she says, hard as the edges of the bulbous jade on her right hand. The ring looks real.

'You don't live here,' I say. Her eyebrows pitch up suddenly.

'No.' She shrugs, as if deciding that this particular fact bears no weight. 'Of course not.'

Leaning forward, the dust in the air mingling with the powder on her chest, she fixes me with a steely stare. 'I'm losing interest. Tell me who you are and what you want or I'll make things ugly. You don't throw that name around lightly.'

As she speaks, she moves her face so close I can see the bleeding edge of her painted mouth. Inexplicably, it makes me shudder.

'Lois Slattery,' I say quickly. 'She worked for you?'

She doesn't respond but looks ready to say or do something that I am pretty sure I won't like. I know I have to move quickly.

'She's dead,' I say. 'Murdered. Don't you care?'

She leans back, pursing her lips and nearly curling herself into a purring smile.

'That no-count bitch. How do you know I didn't kill her myself? She caused me enough trouble.'

'You didn't,' I say, suddenly realizing I have no idea if she did. 'But you know things.'

Her back stiffens. 'You better have a bankroll the size of my fist if you want that kind of information.'

'No bankroll. But something that might be worth more.' I reach into my pocket and pull out Joe Avalon's address book. The book that has been sitting in my dresser for months.

I can tell from the hitch in her eyes that

she recognizes it on sight. In a flash, however, she puts on a poker face.

'Is this where the music rises and I clasp my chest like Kay Francis?' She is tough, but she shows more than she means to. She wants the book.

'You need to tell me everything you know about Lois and what happened to her,' I say coolly. 'And then you get this. And you don't need to waste my time. I know you know what it is.'

'Is that so–'

'Now *I'm* losing interest.' I feign brusqueness, gathering my gloves and bag. 'I know other people who will give me information *and* a fat bankroll to boot for this.'

She sighs, eyes continually darting toward the address book.

'What good does that book do me? I don't need addresses, phone numbers.'

This is what I am afraid of. Is that all the book contains? Even with its funny code? The shorthand that I can't crack?

'I think you know it's more than that,' I bluff.

'Let me see it.'

'I'm listening,' I say, leaning back for effect, even as I feel the sofa's dust seal itself to my back.

She pauses, running her pointy fingers from her throat to her ample cleavage.

'Fine. Fine. Slattery. A no-good whore.

What else do you need to know?'

'You're going to have to do better than that.'

'She was a party girl. I take care of party girls. They stay here when they need to. They get taken care of' – she gestures ominously to the bedroom – 'when they need to. Lois was one of dozens. She was especially popular because she was especially ... agreeable. Some girls have rules. Lois had no rules.'

Suddenly, her cool breaks, for a split second. Her face visibly darkens. 'No rules,' she murmurs grimly, looking down at her hands.

Shaking herself out of it, she continues, 'Girls like that don't end well. She must have made the wrong date.'

'She had a date the night she was killed?'

'That book in your hand better be damn good,' she says coldly. 'Come here.'

She rises and wearily walks me over to the door adjacent to the bedroom. Stepping in, I see a small room dominated by a large, sagging bookshelf.

'Girls leave things here. When they're flopping. They leave valuables, personal items. I let them,' she says, reaching down to the bottom shelf. She grabs a large shoe box that has 'Lois' scrawled across it in loopy script. I guess I've never seen Lois's child-like scribble.

I take the box from her outstretched hands.

'Didn't the police seize this?' I ask, before thinking.

'They're looking for Linda Tattersal, wherever Lois got that name. They haven't been here. They don't know anything.' She eyes me frostily. 'Do they?'

'Not as far as I know. Which is good luck for us both,' I say. I carry the box back into the living room and open it.

Somehow I thought it would contain revelations, by magic some proof – like a photograph of her own murder.

The first thing I see is a gold shell compact I recognize as my own. I had presumed it lost months ago. There are a handful of swizzle sticks from places like Dynamite Jackson's and Café Society. In one corner a sticky-looking syringe has wedged itself.

'That can't be any surprise,' Mrs. MacMurray growls. 'She didn't just use. She booted it.'

'She what?'

'She booted it – hit the needle real slow, pulling back and pumping the blood again and again to get a bigger fix. Tough stuff, that one. And I only know tough.'

A few lipsticks roll from one end of the box to the other. I notice a small, pocket-size pad of mauve paper beneath the syringe and slide it out.

'That's the idea,' Mrs. MacMurray says blankly, one eye searching for the address book, which I have temporarily returned to my pocket.

It is a list of hotels and motels and nightclubs, as far as I can tell. Next to each is a set of initials. The printing is in neat black grease pencil.

'Favorite haunts of her regulars. Hard to keep them straight. I told her to log them to help her remember which name to call out.'

'These are just initials.'

'And those are just numbers and addresses, right?' she says, pointing to the address book.

I scan the list quickly, looking for the Rest E-Z Motel. If any of Lois's dates were dangerous, that was one of them.

On the third page, there it is: 'Rest E-Z: WS.'

'Walter Schor,' I say out loud, remembering Mike's comment about Joe Avalon's main studio client.

'Why not? Walter Schor, William Shakespeare. Why not look for Louis B. Mayer in there while you're at it? Darryl Zanuck.'

'You want this?' I finger the address book.

'You want this?' She reaches into her robe pocket and pulls out a small, shiny revolver. The gesture is so cinematic that I feel no fear. Just a cold rush of adrenaline.

'You don't want to use that. You would

have used it already if that's what you wanted.'

She smiles lightly. 'Sure, I don't want to use it. That's not a mess I want to clean up. Look, I'm a lying, cheating grifter. But I play fair, within reason. I promised you information for the book. I've given you all you need. Now give me the book and you can take that box and get it far, far away from me. I've washed my hands of her. She stains badly, little girl. I don't need it.'

I hand her the book, as happy to be rid of it as she is to be rid of Lois's things. She opens it immediately. As far as she is concerned, I'm already gone.

'Thank you, Mrs. MacMurray,' I say, rising, – tucking the shoe box under my arm. 'I'll show myself out.'

Her eyes tear across the pages as I head toward the door. As I open it, I decide to take one last shot. From over my shoulder, I call out, 'Oh, and where's Alice Steele's box?'

Without looking up, ravenously consuming each mystifying page, she mutters, 'She picked that up long ago.'

It is hours later, with the box set on my tufted bedspread, that I understand why I was so struck by Lois's name on the top. It had been tingling in the back of my head ever since.

The writing in the pad did not match. It

had been written by someone else – maybe Joe Avalon, or likely Mrs. MacMurray herself. As for the scrawled name on the box, I suddenly recognize the hand. The same looping, wavering, slanted scribble.

Your brothers wife is a tramp, she's no good and she'll rune him, if you dont beleve me, ask at the Red room lounge in Holywd.

The postcard of the Santa Monica Pier that had led me to the Red Room Lounge.

Lois had been trying to tell me something. Maybe she lost her nerve once I arrived. Or maybe she was just seeing if I'd bite. Maybe she was showing Alice how close she could get to me. Or maybe, maybe she was looking for help.

If WS was Walter Schor and he was the man who had beaten up Lois, it wasn't hard to believe he was the type of man who could also have killed her. I wonder if Alice knew and if she did, why she didn't do anything about it. And if she didn't, then why she was content to let Lois just disappear.

I think of Lois's torn body at the Rest E-Z Motel. I think of the look in her eyes, of despair and wry defeat, or provocation and surrender. She wanted me to *see*, to know the kind of world she – and by extension, Alice – lived in. Was she blackmailing Alice or just refusing Alice her own escape?

Pushing aside my doubts from the night before, I call Mike.

'Can you tell me something about Walter Schor?'

'Sure. What are you looking for, sweetheart?'

'Would he be the type who would hurt women?'

He doesn't even pause. 'No, no. He's not the one you're looking for, Lora. You're on the wrong track. Besides, I heard that Lois was running up and down Central Avenue every night. Far more likely this has to do with drugs and a bad scene.'

The feeling I had in the file room as he snapped up Lois's file folder returns, but with more intensity – a bristling up my spine, rough as a razor. 'When did you hear this?'

'Asking around. She was moving in a very rough crowd. These things happen.'

'What's wrong?' I nearly gulp, straining for air. When Mike saw Olive MacMurray's name in Lois's file, he somehow figured it all out. Figured out that this wasn't just about Alice and a two-bit thug like Joe Avalon, an easily replaceable pimp. This went higher, sunk deeper. He is lost to me.

'Wrong?'

'You sound different from last night, at my apartment.'

'Different? No, baby, not different. Listen, I had an idea. How about you and me and a drive up the coast this weekend? Or Catalina and all that? Get our minds off all this. Forget about it.'

I try to get some control of my voice. I want to sound casual. I want to sound like nothing is wrong.

'That sounds wonderful, Mike. But I've got a lot of work to do this weekend, stacks of student papers and lesson plans. Listen, I'll call you later.'

'Okay. What are you doing tomorrow?'

'Just cleaning house,' I say as I hang up. I am going to have to do it alone.

Lois lying, facedown, in dark water. Born only to die and to die like this, lost, forgotten, brutalized, released, left faceless, nameless, alone. Somebody had to speak for her. That night, I dream of her. Of her speaking to me. Hair twisted with seaweed, face swimming out of dark water, eyes imploring, mouth coiled darkly, queerly into a smile. *Lora,* she would say, *Lora, you know more than you think. You know everything.*

These are the things I barely remember: Calling in sick. Driving to my bank. Waiting twenty minutes for it to open. Withdrawing my savings – only four hundred dollars, but a world of effort for me. Driving back to the ghostly house on Manchester, the long, long drive past countless streets baroque and scarred, nondescript and ominous.

The next thing I know I am looking at Olive MacMurray's startled expression as she peers at me from around the corner of the sofa, ten feet and a screen door separating us.

There must be something in my eyes, something hanging there, dangling dangerously, because she stands, not moving closer, only hissing faintly, 'What are you doing here?'

'I need to see you.'

'We finished our business,' she says in clipped, hushed tones, stripped of the prior day's wile.

'I have money. I need to know some things about Alice Steele.'

She rushes to the door, her face stretched tight, and hastily ushers me in with trembling hands. 'Listen, you, you don't know what you've gotten yourself into. I don't want any part of this.'

'What do you mean? What happened?'

'How much do you have?' She twists her fingers anxiously.

'Four hundred dollars. But only if you can answer all my questions.'

She waves me over to the sofa. Someone has gotten to her. Joe Avalon has gotten to her. I feel my teeth set on edge.

'I'll take that money. I need that money now.' The powdered flesh of her bosom mottled today, her hands clenching.

'Who wrote Lois's schedule of dates? Was that you?'

'No. It was your sister-in-law,' she snaps.

'Why?' I snap back, only then realizing what she has said:

Your sister-in-law. She knows who I am, maybe has known all along. But there is no time for this revelation. I repeat, 'Why?'

She takes a deep breath, then, 'She was one of the girls, fancy ambitions but dangerous habits. She had an arrangement with Avalon. She helped control Lois. Helped keep her jumping – Lois and her big mouth. Joe wanted to dump her or worse, and Alice kept her alive. She was her lucky piece, as they say.'

'I guess she couldn't keep her alive forever,' I murmur, my head throbbing.

'Once Alice hooked up with her lawman, she had more of an interest in keeping herself in the pink. Lois was a drag on her. It turned out pretty lucky for Alice in the end. But her loose ends may trip us all up yet,' she says, wringing her hands over and over.

I pull the Santa Monica Pier postcard from my pocket.

'Did Lois write this?'

'How should I know?'

'The handwriting?'

'Could be. Lots of the girls write like that.' She reads the card more closely. 'Ah, I get it. She was looking to have something over Alice's head. A bargaining chip.'

'You think Walter Schor killed Lois.'

'I cleaned her up enough times after dates with him,' she says, voice lowering. 'And this sure is worth that four hundred: He sent another one of my girls to the hospital after a night of monkeyshines.'

'Because ... because...' I wonder if I can ask it. 'Because Alice would never ... never hurt Lois.' I couldn't look the woman in the eye.

'I gave up long ago guessing what people were capable of,' she says. 'But my money's on Schor. Question is, How many times did Alice need to put Lois in harm's way before the party girl turned up cold? And I do know this. And then I'm done. Joe Avalon isn't about to be a patsy. And *he's* capable of just about anything when his back is against the wall.'

Her eyes meet mine, and I feel something very weighty has been communicated to me – but its full meaning is as yet unclear.

'It was Joe Avalon?'

She shakes her head. 'You're missing it. Listen close, and then I'm closing the shutters on the information booth. Joe Avalon isn't about to be a patsy. And, *right now*, he's capable of just about anything.

'By the way,' she adds, rising. 'It was Alice Steele, couple years back, who got put in the hospital at Walter Schor's hands. You don't forget that kind of dinner date.

'Before we took her in to County, she spent two days in there' – she gestures to the bedroom– 'filling it with blood.'

I park my car three doors down from Olive MacMurray's house, trying to unravel all she said for my four hundred dollars. I don't trust myself to drive yet.

I sit for about twenty minutes thinking about Lois and why she let herself fall into Walter Schor's poisonous arms over and over again – one long death scene. *The kind of dance you're lucky to make it out of,* she'd said, not so lucky herself.

And I think of Alice, Alice serving herself up to countless men and now sunk deep, heels dug in, in my brother's home. And Alice once lying on that bed in that fetid house, lying there, body twitching, more blood with each spasm, more pain with every move. Lying there in a doomed attempt to hide, to hide this, to hide all this. And it was to hide, to conceal, to bury, that she sent Lois up to the pyre and watched as the flames ate her alive.

My God, Bill, what you've let crawl into your bed … you poor, hapless thing … must you pay so much for your fine innocence?

I sit for about twenty minutes
I sit for about twenty minutes and then
It is then and there it is. There is no one there, and suddenly, blinking back at the house, I see him flicker up Olive Mac-Murray's porch steps out of the corner of my eye.

I have his picture in my head and then he is there. And me Like a sleepwalker
As someone hypnotized
And there I am, now out of my car, fast and without thinking, slinking past the three houses
Back to 551706 Manchester
Walking in a silence so deep it is as if all sound has been sucked out of the world
I walk along the side of the house
lean up against the wall, against the pitted shingles
along the window, open, paint-flecked
through all this I pretend I didn't see *who I saw,* pretend it was just a trick of the light, the eye
like the old adage, Speak of the devil, and he shall appear
I press my hand, my palm against the heat-curled shingles
I might have even whispered it aloud
not Bill it couldn't be Bill not my brother not
then I hear the voice through the screen window

'We're talking a lot of money here,' he says. 'And all the protection you could want.'

Could that hard, anxious sound possibly be my brother's voice?

'How much money? My life wouldn't be worth a plug nickel, Detective.'

'He wouldn't be able to touch you, Mrs. MacMurray. I can promise that. We're talking serious money.'

'I'd need five grand.'

'Fine. I'll arrange to have it wired to your bank account this afternoon.'

'Do I look like a landlady? I don't have a bank account.'

'I'll get it to you.' A quaver tilts into his voice, and *it is Bill and my God—*

'He's going to find out I gave him up to you.'

'He won't. And if he does, it won't matter. He'll be in county jail and then prison for life. Murder first-degree conviction for Avalon. I promise.'

'And I get all his girls. And I get all his studio johns.'

'Right. Who else but you?'

'I suppose even Walter Schor, if I want him.'

'Because you've got what I need to pin this on Avalon?' Hot desperation in his voice.

'We can make it work. He's dirty enough for any frame to work.'

'He's an animal.' Quaver gone and now a

254

hard bark. 'I got into the law to beat guys like this.' *Oh, it is horrible.*

'Whatever you say, copper,' a low, amused drawl.

A loud noise, a sound like a blood howl and it is me?

As I watch him walk rapidly out of the house, my body begins moving too. He passes his car and keeps going until he reaches the donut shop. I follow at a distance. *Don't think about it now, don't think about it now, just find out how, why, anything you can.*

Looking furtively to his right and left – my *brother, like a criminal* – he ducks into the phone booth out front. I move quickly around the back of the shop and then sidle along the far wall, inching as close as I can to the front of the building while still remaining hidden by both the corner and the meager hedgerow that wraps around it. He has shut the phone booth door, but I can still hear.

His voice is loud, raked raw. 'I did it. Don't worry. I took care of it. I told you I would.'

His effort to control his voice, sound strong is painful.

'No,' he says. 'It's just like I promised. She'll pin him for it. She'll claim he came to her that night talking about how he'd dumped her in the canyon. She'll say he did it to keep her in line. She'll say Lois was terrified of him. Once she has the money, she'll tell more.'

He pauses for a moment, listening. Listening and, I can hear it, jabbing his fist rhythmically against the door of the booth.

'Yes, yes. I did it all. You know, Alice, you know, he's done enough bad things he never got caught for. So he can pay by paying for this. He can pay for this. He should pay. This is about the kind of man he is and those things he made you do. He can't hurt you anymore.'

He can't stop. He isn't talking to her. He doesn't know it, but he's talking to me.

'He's going to pay for the things he made you do.'

I want to protect you from all that, my brother Bill once said to me. I had returned home crying. Some boy who had cornered me in his car, pressed himself so close, so roughly his watch had caught on my sweater and snagged it from collarbone to waist. The sweater was a favorite, was the perfect aquamarine. It was the softest thing I'd ever owned. It felt like pussy willows against my skin. It was the ruined sweater that brought me home with tears stinging. But my brother assumed it was the boy.

—Did he hurt you? Did he force himself on you?

—He tried to. He kept … trying.

It was true, after all.

It took nearly an hour to persuade him not to go to this boy's house. I knew he wouldn't hurt the boy, just frighten him, scold him. But I was too embarrassed. And part of me would rather listen to him. Listen to him say things like

—I want to protect you from all that. I don't want you to have to know these things. About men. I want you to be safe forever. I will make you safe forever.

I want to protect you.

From somewhere in the dark murk of my head, the phone jumps at me.

'Lora? It's Bill. I'm glad you're there. We've been kind of worried about you. Alice says you missed school today.'

Images of my brother at Olive MacMurray's that very afternoon crackle through my head. I can't remember anything else I have done in the last six hours. Did I really drive home, park my car, walk up the stairs to my apartment, pour the glass of water in front of me, light the cigarette – whose cigarette? – I seem to be smoking now?

Gathering myself, stopping my pounding heart with my hand, pulling on a face, a voice, I say: 'I wasn't feeling well.'

'Well, we thought maybe you forgot about the party. It starts soon.'

'Party?'

'The charity event Alice is hosting, remember? For the Police Benevolent League?'

'Right.' I vaguely remember agreeing to bring a tray of rumaki.

'People are supposed to get here in half an hour.'

'I'll be there,' I say.

I say it as though nothing has happened. And then it becomes as though nothing has happened. My brother is the same. I am the same. Somehow we've all agreed. It is the only way to go forward, to speak, to move. I can do it. There is some strange steel to me.

I open the refrigerator door. I don't have any chicken livers for the rumaki, so water chestnuts will have to do. As I stand wrapping the bacon around each piece, sliding in a pineapple chunk, my mind keeps shuttling back to seeing Bill again, how I'll see his face and know. Know what? There is nothing to know.

I set my jaw, focus my eyes.

The busier I make myself with the food, the slippery pineapple and the frilly toothpicks and the sticky honey glaze on my fingers, the more I am able to send myself back to my Bill, the Bill who never surprises me except with the extent of his flinty decency, his goodness, his deathless integrity.

The more I think of this, the more I think of what he might do for me if I were so ensnared. The more I think of this, wrapping the rumaki in wax paper, the more the fog in my head clears, my thinking becomes razor-sharp. I can go to the party and I can see what she has brought upon him, what she has brought him to. I can look the damage in the face and then I will know what to do.

The staggering thing is this: amid everything, amid all Alice's efforts to conceal a murder, to entrap her husband in the treachery, to bribe one partner in crime and frame the other, she still manages to orchestrate another one of her extravagant spectacles.

Japanese lanterns have been artfully positioned to spread a pink haze everywhere, over the platters of egg rolls and plum sauce, fried wontons, fortune cookies, glistening pork on bamboo skewers, and the tureen of chow mein, over the tall vases filled with moon lilies and bamboo stalks, the hanging temple bells tingling serene music from the patio, over the sandalwood fan party favors in the basket by the door, the paper dragon stretched across the fireplace. It is pitch perfect. It is almost obscene.

And there is Alice, her dark hair pulled back tight and her eye makeup straight out of a Charlie Chan movie, emerging from under one of the cherry blossom parasols on the patio in a searing turquoise cheongsam dress, all the rage since Jennifer Jones wore one in *Love Is a Many Splendored Thing*.

As she moves across the room to greet me, I feel a hard chill drag down my spine. Can I really do this, be here, see them? It is as though time has slowed to a hypnotic crawl as she makes her way toward me, the silk of her cheongsam shushing, her feet, in wooden sandals, making no sound on the thick carpet, her head lowered like a good geisha. Then, as she approaches me, her darkly lined lids rise and she looks at me and in that look...

In that look, perhaps for the first time since I've known her, she conceals nothing. Her gaze – filled with rage, terror, shame, ugliness, and still, her keen beauty – scissors through me, and I feel I have been gored.

'Lora! And you remembered the rumaki,' she coos with a kind of honeyed slither. 'I can always count on you.'

I can't speak, can't bear to, then–

'Sis.'

I feel the familiar warm, heavy arm on my shoulder, and something in me, something held tight, collapses.

'Hi, Bill.' I can't look up at him. I merely feel him, smell his old-fashioned aftershave, the scent of which is pressed, warm and peppery, into everything he owns.

And then they are both gone, people coming in behind me and Alice whisking my platter off to the kitchen.

It is only then that I notice the dozen guests already in the room, drinking Singapore slings and mai tais, the women waving their fans languorously and the men lighting cigarettes and the Four Aces crooning, 'Your fingers touched my silent heart and taught it how to sing,' on the stereo and everything going on as if nothing...

I float around the space like a ghost, avoiding conversations, speaking to no one, trying to disappear into the crimson haze of the decor.

Looking at Alice from across the room, I see that, although her face is powdered an impeccable white, a faint sheen of perspiration is beginning to pearl on her skin. She is laughing and talking and mixing drinks and adjusting the lanterns as men's heads hit them, but she isn't pulling off the performance with her usual élan. And it both thrills and frightens me.

As for Bill ... Bill is no good at all, half-hiding in a corner chair, continually, compulsively running his hand through his hair, rubbing his jaw until it turns red, tugging at his pants legs, reaching for his drink and then changing his mind and returning his hand to his knee, to his ear, which he tugs, to his tie, which he loosens, then straightens, then loosens and straightens again. Oh God, Bill.

The things I heard him say, only hours before, to that woman, that horrible woman:

'We're talking a lot of money here. And all the protection you could want.'

'...you've got what I need to pin this on Avalon?'

But then I look back at him, at the tightness around his eyes like when, like when there's things going wrong, things he can't control. *Like when a masher grabbed me in the movie theater or when a teacher scolded me in front of the class or when my grandparents pillaged my forbidden box of Dubarry face powder and the only bottle of perfume I'd ever had – Soul of Violet – or when ... or when ... a very bad and dangerous criminal slipped just out of reach.*

I reach over to the bar cart and pour myself a small glass from the first bottle I touch. The feel of it fresh in my throat, I walk across the room to him.

He just wants to save us all, I think. It sends him down some very dark alleys. He can't help it. He never could.

'Hi.'

He looks up at me and when he does
And when he does and I can't forget this
it is with unbearably guilty eyes.

I think I might burst into tears.

'Sis,' he says scratchily, one hand to my arm, soft. 'I'm glad you're here.'

This is what he is really saying: *I had to do it, Lora. Otherwise, it all would have meant nothing.*

And suddenly I understand.

Then, he averts his eyes from mine, rises, and walks away.

I think I might die.

Moving past guests, pretending not to hear anyone who might call my name, I step out onto the empty patio and around the corner to a darker patch of the small yard. A shot of brisk air tingles on my face, and I take another long drink.

'I didn't think you'd show.'

Jumping, I turn and, through the growing dark, make out Mike Standish leaning against the jacaranda tree, hands in his deep linen pockets.

'Likewise,' I say, catching my breath.

'Well, as you know, I've always been a great supporter of law enforcement.'

Peering through the tree's feathery leaves, I think I can see him smiling. He makes no move to indicate he plans on coming out from the shadows.

'Why are you here?'

'I've been asking myself that a lot lately. Almost every time you ask it of me, King.'

'I can't talk to you,' I say, my chin faintly

trembling. I remind myself that everything he says is at least half a lie.

'Why not,' he replies, cool as ever.

'I can't talk to you at all.' I feel my hands jerking, and surprising myself, I see that this moment may in fact be about Mike and Mike and me and I can't do it, not now, and I feel the supple, insinuating warmth of his voice as he says my name and I want him to come out from the shadow of the tree, but I'm afraid if he does, I will be lost.

(One thing, Lora, one thing, Alice had said, he warns you that he's going to charm you, and that warning becomes part of his charm.)

'Just stay away,' my voice, somehow, rings out.

'You think you know things, but you don't.' At last, he steps out of the heavy darkness of the low black branches.

For the first time since I met him I can almost see a path of stubble, a slight wrinkle of the collar, a hair out of place. It's heartbreaking.

'King – *Lora,* you don't know anything. At least not where I'm concerned,' he says.

This is too much. Something slips in me and there's no going back. 'Don't come any closer!' I say, my voice at a higher timbre than I'd meant.

Mike's eyes widen and he stops short.

Out of nowhere, a hand on my shoulder.

'Is he bothering you?' And it is Bill's taut,

broken voice.

Before I even turn around, I feel it in the blood. I feel him straining against his own skin, so desperate for something to fix, to make right. *If I'm not this, then what am I?*

I turn and look up at him. Both these men and their creased white collars and scruffy faces and this is not how it is supposed to be...

'Perfect.' Mike shakes his head.

'No, no,' I say quickly to my brother. I can't manage him, too.

'Do you want me to get him out of here? I will, Lora. What do you want, Lora?' Bill stutters, unsure, never looking at me, looking only at Mike, jaw newly set. 'What has he done?'

What has he done? What have they all done to us both, Bill?

'Skip it,' Mike mutters, seamlessly lighting up a cigarette. 'I was heading out anyway. The police don't need my support these days.'

I put my hand to my mouth at the insinuation and turn my eyes away. Does he know, too? Does he know about my brother, too?

'You know, they take care of themselves now,' Mike adds – needlessly – tossing his match behind him.

As I watch, arms to my sides and mouth slightly open, he walks away, around the side of the house, disappearing into the trapped darkness there.

I turn back around even as I know Bill too is gone, swallowed up by the party, by Alice, or just not wanting to look me in the face.

Inside, everyone is dancing, waiting for Alice to take her usual position at the center, leading the group. But instead she keeps vanishing into the kitchen or the back bedroom or the powder room, a cigarette always in hand, the sweat now coating her skin, seeping into the white geisha girl powder, scattering her black eye makeup.

'Alice! C'mon! Alice, are we going to mambo?'

'Let's go, Alice! We don't know any Oriental dances, unless you count the cha-cha-chopsticks!'

She begs off, mouths an excuse, heads back into the kitchen.

'Bill's in there, too,' I hear Tom Moran bark to two other cops. 'Washing dishes! In the middle of a party!'

Doris Day's voice belts out, 'Oh, why did I tell you it was bye-bye for Shanghai? I'm even allergic to rice...'

'For God's sake, Alice,' someone shouts out. 'We need you.'

I turn around to see that Tom Moran and Chet Connor each have one of Alice's arms and are walking her to the center of the makeshift dance floor.

The look in her eyes is that of a cornered animal, but she quickly reassembles, and inhaling hard, she hoists a dazzling red Alice-smile on her face.

'All right, boys, all right. You can't take no for an answer.'

'Or so Tom's girlfriends say,' Chet guffaws, grabbing Alice around the waist and into position.

All cherries and foamy milk, Doris Day prattles on, 'Why don't you stop me when I talk about Shanghai? It's just a lover's device...'

Alice leans back and grabs a fan from the basket as Chet twirls her. Her distracted look evaporates, and as she twists her wrist and spreads the green fan out in sync with the music, I can see her pleasure, blunt and maddening.

'Who's gonna kiss me? Who's gonna thrill me? Who's gonna hold me tight?...'

Chet laughs delightedly, and everyone steps back to let them have the floor. Eyes glittering, Alice begins singing along, the sultry counterpoint to Doris, 'I'm right around the corner in a phone booth and I want to be with you *tonight!*' Every line Doris belts with cheery vim, Alice matches with tantalizing venom. Everyone is clapping and cheering, packed tight together, maybe twenty-five of them, to see the show.

I feel caught between admiration, awe,

and fury. Whipping around the room, fan snapping and hips swiveling in the tight dress, she's utterly alive, and even when her eyes pass over me, they practically spark with unabated energy, and then, as the last stanza begins..

She almost trips. She's looking, eyelashes shuttered open wide, past me and to the left, at the door.

Her face is sliding off.

That's what it looks like, because it *is*.

I jerk my head around to see what she's looking at, what has so dissembled her. Peering through the throng and smoke, I think I see– And then I see it is.

There is a man standing in the vestibule.

I fix on the lightning bolt scar over his left eye. It's the boy from the studio. The one who drove Joe Avalon. The tough kid seated four chairs down from me as I waited. Teddy. That is his name.

Alice's eyes fix on him for a split second. Only I – and probably Teddy – see. And she finishes the final twirl and then, trying glamorously to catch her breath, clutching her hand to her chest with all the drama of Belle Davis, she fashions a breathtaking smile.

I look back at Teddy, and by the time I turn around again, Alice is gone.

Pushing past the energized dancers, I try to get to Teddy, not knowing what I can possibly say to him. But he has already thrust through the other way, to the patio doors, presumably after Alice.

I squeeze through the oblivious revelers and out the doors, but by the time I'm outside I can't see Alice or Teddy or anyone.

I begin thinking. Avalon sent Teddy here to scare Alice, or abduct her, or worse. He knows she's setting him up. He will do anything he can to stop her. Alice has to have known that this would happen, that Joe would find out about the frame. What's her plan now?

In my head, flashbulbs smash in front of me, and Bill is squinting, covering his face, running down the City Hall steps. *Cop Fired in Disgrace, D.A. to Prosecute His Own.*

On a guess, the only guess left, I walk quickly and purposefully back through the house and into Alice and Bill's bedroom.

I have no idea what I might find. None at all.

Some part of me is sure she is too smart for this, too smart for me. There can be nothing to find. She has spent a life covering her tracks. Passing time in one darkened hotel room after the next, peeling masks off only to expose other, still brighter masks beneath. She knows how to leave no trace.

But time is running out, and I have to take the chance that she is scared and desperate. As it turns out, I am lucky.

It is almost too easy. There in the drawer of the bedside table is an oblong envelope with a drawing of chocolate-colored natives on it, flowers in their hair.

I sit down on the bed and open it. It is the itinerary for a boat trip – the SS *Tarantha* – headed to Brazil. Mr. and Mrs. King. Mr. and Mrs.

The boat leaves tomorrow at six o'clock.

I feel my stomach rise. *How could he go with her?*

I stare at the envelope for several minutes. Then I walk over to the closet and open the top drawer of the tall highboy inside. In it is the dainty Walther PPK pistol Bill brought back from Europe. I put it in my purse.

I'd like to say I have everything planned, but I am just running by pure instinct, some throbbing voice inside me saying, *Don't take any chances.*

I exit the bedroom unseen and leave quickly through the patio door and the black, echoey yard. As I do, I think I might see Teddy lurking in a far corner. I half-expect to see his fleshy scar, feel his hard arms.

For two hours, I drive mindlessly, unable to think. I drive out of Pasadena and its endless, pungent groves all the way to the Sepulveda Dam, all quivering cottonwoods and glittering sycamores, and the new golf course carved in the middle, and then back through Burbank, by the blazing Hollywood Bowl. I drive and as I drive, slowly, with the radio mourning haunted hearts, I find I'm making plans.

Finally, I find myself on my block and then at my building. As I walk from my car, I hear someone walking briskly to catch up with me. I turn with a start, waiting for the lightning bolt, or Joe Avalon's coal-eyed stare. Lately, it seems like I am always turning with a start.

'Detective Cudahy,' I blurt, not entirely relieved.

'You're not playing straight, even after our little talk,' he says with a creeping coldness in his voice.

'I don't know what you mean.'

'Where's your sister-in-law?'

I guess there are few secrets left. I lock eyes with him. He looks tired, frustrated, impatient. 'Where is she, Miss King?'

In my head, I start to say, *Sister-in-law? I don't know what you mean.* But I can't bear to keep playing. I can't stomach putting on the front.

So instead I say, 'I don't know. I came here looking for her.'

He looks slightly relieved at my bluntness. 'She knew we were closing in. We were tailing her.'

'And you lost her?'

'She lost us. I was staking out the party and she just disappeared. One minute she was there, the next she was gone. Must have left on foot. We're guessing she's on her way into hiding, or skipped town. This may come as a big surprise to you, Miss King, but she knows even more than you.'

'I thought maybe,' I say, inwardly relieved. He has figured out a lot, but not everything.

And then he pauses as if deciding something.

'We'll keep your brother out of it,' he finally says, nodding toward me.

I feel my eye twitch. I don't know why I wasn't expecting him to mention Bill. I don't know why I thought Bill was still safe.

I consider, fleetingly, telling him about the tickets to Brazil. But I have no real reason to believe Cudahy would, or could, keep my brother out of it. And, more pressingly, I have no reason to believe Bill would, or could, stay out of it.

'We know he doesn't know what he married into,' Cudahy continues. 'The circles your sister-in-law moved in.'

'Right.'

'You should have told me about him. About who you were.'

'I know.'

As I walk up the stairs, my head is blank. It crosses my mind that I can't be sure I'm not being followed now. Still, what choice do I have? I have to take my chances.

When I enter the apartment, the phone is ringing. Somehow I know it has been ringing for hours.

'It's Alice. Don't you think it's time we spoke?' I hear the roar of the ocean in the background.

I say, 'Where?' and she tells me.

On the long drive to meet Alice, I am careful to watch my rearview mirror. I take some winding detours and don't notice anyone.

I am thinking that there are so many things about Alice that I will never know. An airless gap between the stories of her low-rent childhood and her years working for studio costume departments. And do I even know if these exotically sketched narratives are true?

She made herself into someone you didn't ask questions of because somehow you didn't know the right questions to ask. Or the questions you wanted to ask seemed impossibly naïve in the face of the dark maw that lay behind her finely etched wife face.

Once I thought she was trying to escape a darkness, and she found rescue in Bill. Now I know that she wanted both. She liked the double life. It kept her alive.

I arrive at Miramar Point as the moon shows its full size, giving off a faint glitter on the water, whose waves cream forward into sleek spit curls before straightening out to stretched silk again. A lone boat knocks around the Santa Monica breakwater. Past it, the colossal gap of the ocean hangs a steely purple.

I park on a small ridge off the highway and make my way to the top of an endless flight of wooden steps. My hand moist on the nickel rail as I ascend higher and higher, I make the final turn to reach the restaurant. Its round booths, hung over with fairy lights, are uninhabited except for a young man with a shock of white-blond hair nodding off over his drink. A cat twined at his feet suddenly arches his back at me as I walk over and slide into a booth, ordering a short glass of red wine.

It is twenty minutes before I hear someone call. Looking out, I see her making her way up the long set of steps.

Through the brown-violet dusk, I can see her waving, waving as if somehow – against all reason – glad to see me.

As she walks up the last stretch, I think of nothing but the faint sound of passing cars on the highway below. It is the only way.

Moments later, we are leaning, small

glasses of anisette in hand, over the terrace rail behind the bar. Her hair, long and undone, swirls around her as she turns to face me. Every moment feels unutterably significant.

'Remember that night when I told you I felt like someone was following me?' she says evenly.

Before I can say I don't remember it at all, she adds, 'Isn't it funny that it was you?'

Taken aback, I say, 'I'm not following you.'

'No?' she says, and suddenly I'm not so sure.

She taps out the final cigarette from her creased pack, her fingers sallow at the tips.

'It's you who's followed me,' I insist severely. 'Telling Mike Standish things that you couldn't know.'

She only smiles.

'You wanted to scare me off this. But you can't.' I feel my nerve rise the more I speak. If she wants it straight, I'll give it to her. 'Why did you keep letting Lois go to Walter Schor when you knew the kind of man–'

I wasn't expecting the response.

'Why not?' Her eyes ringed red. 'If it wasn't him, it would have been someone else. Girls like us–' she begins, then lifts her shoulders almost in a shrug. The *us* is painfully, devastatingly vague.

'But you were out of it all. You could have been out.'

'There is no out.' Her eyes like fresh teeth, hooking into me. 'Don't you know?'

I ignore her question, try once again to shift the conversation to the immediate, the practical.

'So Mike told you,' I say. 'What I'd found out.' I'm not sure if it is a question or not. The conversation feels unreal, unmoored. I feel drunk, nerves hot and tingling.

'Everything. He told me everything,' she says, and runs a finger along her lips, blue under the lights. 'He couldn't help it. He had to give me all of it. He was in love and he couldn't distinguish.'

'In love.'

'With you, my girl. I figured on a lot, but not on that.' She draws in the smoke.

'I should have,' she adds, almost kindly. The tone sets something off in me.

'Why don't you just tell me. Why don't you just tell me. Was it you? Did you kill her.' My voice is like a knot unloosing too fast, uncontrollable. Even as I say it, I don't really believe it. But I want to see. I want to see how bad it is.

'I didn't kill her.' Alice shakes her head. 'But I might have, it's true. If I had to. She knew I couldn't leave everything behind. Not everything. Or couldn't yet. I still liked the perfume of it, even if I sometimes hated myself for it.

'Walter Schor, you know all about him, I

guess? She showed up at his house. She knew you were never supposed to do that. She wasn't following any of the rules anymore. Schor called us both. Said get her out of here or there's going to be trouble. He was through with her anyway.

'When Joe and I got there, his flunkies, they said they didn't know where she was. But you could feel something in the air, something awful.

'We kept looking through the entire house, walking down corridor after corridor, in and out of over a half dozen bedrooms and sitting rooms and a projection room and pantries and a room, Lora, a room just for arranging flowers.

'The longer it took to find her, the more we both saw our futures shuddering before us. He could see trouble with cops and all the bad business that comes with it. I could see worse. The end of everything.

'It was a half hour before we found her. We'd already looked at his famous saltwater pool and hadn't seen her. But when I was upstairs in one of the bedrooms, I stepped out on a balcony and looked down at the big kidney shape, and there was something in it, floating.

'It looked like a big black rose, like those aerial shots in old musicals, round black-stockinged chorus girl legs fanning out into big flowers.'

She spreads her blue-lit hand out over the water beneath us.

'It was her dress blooming.

'Joe and I ran down, and he kneeled over and he saw too.

'Neither of us jumped in. Isn't that strange?' She turns to me, as if wanting an answer.

I don't say anything. How can I say anything? I look down past the railing, into the surf. I look down and listen to her buzzing, relentless voice.

'And, Lora, it was so funny. Lois was leaning over herself, facedown, curled over like the top of a cane. Joe reached out and tugged her toward the pool's edge. I can still see him lifting her head up. Her eyes were wide open. I wasn't expecting that. They were beautiful.

'Before I passed him off to Lois, I was Schor's girl for a long time, with the scars to show for it. He wasn't even as rough as they come. I've had rougher. But I knew it could have been me. In many ways, it was me: Alice Steele, folded up upon herself, and Alice King waiting there, ready to cut her losses, reborn free of old ties, old stories, old desires...

'Joe called two of his boys and told them to dump her but first make her hard to identify. They didn't do much of a job. They didn't think they needed to. Who would stand up for Lois? Who would even look for her?'

She reaches out and grabs my face in her hand. 'You really want to know?' Her grip is cold marble on my skin. 'Listen' – she holds my chin more tightly, forcing my eyes to hers– 'listen, Lora. Isn't this the kind of thing you've always wanted to know? Isn't this the kind of thing you've been touching with your fingertips since we met? Touching in the dark?'

No.

'They busted a cap together, he beat her raw, and when he was done, he pushed her in, and let her sink like a stone. Maybe he held her under, forcing all that hot dirty life out of her.

'Listen, Lora, listen.'

The way she looks at me – I remember what Mike once said: *She wasn't just a B-girl, she was carrying the whole ugly world in her eyes.*

Then she finishes me off. 'When we got there, Schor was reading the racing form. Drinking cognac and circling sure things with a little blue pencil.'

My hand darts out, knocks her arm away from me forcefully. Then slaps her face with a sharp crack. Her face shoots backward, but she doesn't even blink. I think she might smile.

'Just tell me. My brother–' I start, then feel

all the sound rush out of me – *when did he fall when did he fall so far* – blood beating in my brain. It is too much.

'Of course.' She nods, and now she is smiling but softly, a streak of red seared to her cheek. 'Of course. That's what you really want to know. That's all you really want.'

She shakes her head. 'Lora, that doesn't matter.'

'I don't. I don't,' I say, shaking my head, shaking it loose.

'I came to him when I had no choice left. Bill, he...' She starts, then stumbles.

'He was in love and he couldn't distinguish,' I say, turning away from her, eyes brimming. I say it not for her but for him. Only for him.

We each take a long drink from our glasses. The liqueur snakes down my throat, steeling me.

'I'm not stopping,' I say in a scratchy voice I don't recognize. 'I have to help him. He can't see...'

Her expression turns from loose to tight, a flat mask. 'You'll bring him down. Is that what you want? That bum cop you're spilling to. Joe told me all about him. You do know he'll have your brother's badge. Lock him up and throw away the key. It'll be your fault. Is that what you want?'

I've never heard her talk quite this way, quite this hard.

'Is that what you want?' she prods.

'You – you crashed into him,' I suddenly, incongruously say, then furl my brow. *What am I saying?* The words make no sense.

'I can save him.' I recover. *He's saved me.*

'Listen,' she says, brittle and dangerous. 'The only way you can save him is by letting this go. Just let it get handled and shake the cop off us.'

I feel my hand gripping the rail. I swivel toward her.

You think you can ... infect him. You think you have the right. You have no right. I can protect him from you, from it, from whatever this is that you've tried to ... pollute him with.

I think all this, my head throbbing, vein pulsing in my brain. But my only chance is in her not knowing that I found out about the plan to frame Joe Avalon and, most of all, the plan to leave the next day. I can't let her know that I learned he is risking everything and doing things he'd never, never do.

So all I say is, 'Okay. Okay, Alice Steele.'

He wouldn't tell me at all. He'd just make it go away.

The puckering anisette still in my veins, her voice still hot in my head, I drive straight to the only place where I have a chance, even though it is a slim one.

Parking my car half a block down on Flower Street, I walk quickly to Joe Avalon's house, rehearsing in my head what I will say.

He doesn't seem surprised to see me, even though it is nearly three in the morning.

Not saying a word, he jerks his unshaven jaw to gesture me in, a highball glass in his hand.

Somehow – I would never understand this later – I am not afraid. Not of him, at least.

All the blinds are closed, and I sit on the edge of one of the thick leather chairs.

'Olive told me you might be by,' he says gruffly. 'I can't figure out what you're up to, Miss King. Not for the life of me. I oughta call your fucking brother and threaten you dead if he doesn't stop.'

I think of clever Olive MacMurray playing both sides, working Joe Avalon while agreeing to help frame him.

'You could call him,' I say evenly. 'But I don't think you will.'

'Why not?'

I pull my brother's pistol out of my purse and direct it toward his stomach.

His smudge-circled eyes barely widen. 'You gotta be kidding me,' he mutters. 'I've lost all instinct about you girls.'

'I want to know what happened. To Lois.'

'You aren't going to use that.' He gestures toward the pistol. 'I could get it from you in under a second.'

'Maybe.' I nod. 'But like you said, you've lost all instinct. I think you'd rather be careful. I think you're nothing if not cautious. I'm asking very little.'

He sighs, sitting on the arm of the sofa, resting the glass on his knee. He is a very tired man. All these men are so, so tired.

'I knew Schor might end up doing something like it, but Alice kept saying, Lois can take care of herself. Don't want to lose the butter and egg man.'

'Alice?'

He smiles. 'For toughness, I got nothing on her, honey. You don't even know. I'm a fucking ingenue. Never saw one like it, and that includes three dances in San Quentin. You have no idea.'

'But–'

'Schor did her, but Alice and I, we took care of it. Alice didn't want to stop the gravy train. She was ready to keep Schor happy.'

'Why did she do it?' I demand. 'She had everything. Why didn't she just cut ties?'

He shrugs, his eyes suddenly dreamy. 'Never could explain her. Not that one. She couldn't step out of it. And it served her. But Lois was getting too close. Talking too much. To everyone. To you.'

His eyes turn harder, quite suddenly. 'Those girls, they'd have been nothing without me and they both fucked me. Even if I slip out of this frame, I still gotta leave town.'

'And Edie Beauvais?'

'You know about that one?' He seems almost impressed. 'Alice introduced us. She had a liking for some bad stuff, had been sampling it with Alice, two housewives sitting on the patio in the middle of the day doped up to their pearl necklaces. It ended up getting the best of her. There's no darker story than that, as far as she goes. It was one long suicide.'

'I see.'

I'd never imagined Edie as anything more than the slope of her stomach, waiting to be a mother. To me, she was still Sunday dinners at Charlie's table, flitting around, arms bending under serving dishes. Somehow, that wasn't her, not really, cracked and tilted, on the bathroom floor of the bungalow apartment on Pico Boulevard. One long suicide. All these lost girls...

'Well, Alice and I were cleaning everything up. But then you, little girl.' He points a long finger at me. 'You sicced the law on us. It fucked everything up. The cop you've been dancing with started following me. He was following Alice. I had to start playing for myself, and apparently so did she. But she had the D.A.'s office on her side. At least one member of it. Tough competition. She told her daddy – your brother. Fessed up to a version of the truth, far as I can tell. And what do you know, he's come out guns blazing to save her skin.'

'You don't–'

'Hey.' He leans back, touching his chest lightly with his fingertips. 'Is it my fault your brother developed such a taste for trash? Too many years tunneling through it on the job and it's in him.'

I feel my knuckles shake against the pistol. It is all I can do not to squeeze the trigger. The feeling is so strong that I terrify myself.

'Should I let you out of here?' he continues, not noticing my hand, my quavering fingers. 'How do I know you're not out to fuck me, too? You don't even know how to use that thing.'

'I don't care,' I say, my voice tremulous, eerily wailing like something inhuman, trapped. 'I'll keep pulling the trigger until I get it right.'

He watches me closely. 'I think I know what you could do and what you couldn't.'

'How could you?' I say with a keening hum. 'How could you when *I* don't know?'

I feel an awareness nearly come crashing in.

'Look at what I'm doing. Look at me,' I find myself saying, my face hot.

His eyes fix on mine. In the dark room, I can see them glistening, reading, piercing. I let him see it all. I let him see everything.

He holds my gaze for a long twenty

seconds, then, with a twitch, he shakes it off. Narrowing his eyes suddenly, he barks, 'But I think you got something for me. I think this goes two ways.'

'It will all happen tomorrow.'

My brother's voice, tingling through my head, touching lightly every nerve – no, like ink spreading:

'I had to do it. Otherwise, it meant nothing.'

...like a door shutting somewhere...

I pick up the phone and hold it in my lap for a moment. Then I take a deep breath.

'Gardenia two – five four three five.' I read the number off the small card Joe Avalon has given me.

'One moment.'

I let it ring twelve times. No answer.

I walk around my apartment three times. I wash my face and hands. I stare in the mirror, smoothing my eyebrows, my hair.

I call again.

No answer.

I walk into my kitchen and pull out a mop. I clean the floors with extra bleach. Open a window. Notice the sheen of dust on the sill. Pull out a dust rag and dust every window in the apartment.

I call again.

No answer.

I run the carpet cleaner over the figured rugs. I straighten the shoes in my closet, adjusting the shoe trees. I run down to the lobby to get my mail. It hasn't arrived.

I call again.

'Yeah?' Joe Avalon's voice, but even harder, icier than the night before.

'Are you ready?' It isn't me talking, but someone is talking. Some cool, measured voice with firm enunciation. Fine as piano wire.

'Go.'

'She's going to be at the San Pedro Port, boarding the SS *Tarantha* at 6 P.M.'

And I set the receiver back down on the base curled in my lap.

Later, I remember looking in the mirror for a long time, struck.

I imagine it in advance. My brother's pleading voice.

—I have to go, Lora.

—You said you'd protect me.

—You don't need me now. Alice does. I can save her.

I imagine it and know it won't work, not like that. To make him believe he needs to stay, I have to make it so that he can't leave.

Timing is the linchpin, and luckily I know the schedule. I make several calls to the

D.A.'s office to track Bill's movements. I figure he plans to meet Alice by 5:30, but by then, if everything falls as it should, he will be speeding his way, siren on, to my apartment in far-flung Pasadena.

I go to the Western Union office first and write the telegram to be delivered the following day.

I return to my apartment, mind racing, imagining scenarios, plotting as though I've been living this way my whole life. I look at my watch and wait for the minute hand to strike five minutes to five– the time his shift is supposed to end.

I pick up the phone and dial him.

'Bill.'

'Lora. You just caught me on my way out.' How can he try to sound as if everything is normal, thinking, as he does, that he will be abandoning everything within a few hours?

'Bill, it's over.' I feed a light sob into my voice.

'What? Lora, what's wrong?'

'Don't blame ... don't blame...'

'*Lora.* Is this about Standish? I knew last night... Did he hurt you?'

Out of my mouth, the half-remembered lyric.

'*This, my darling, this is the end of every-thing.*'

And as I hang up, I can hear him say, 'I'll be right there. Don't do anything, Sis. I'll be right there.'

The irony is blissful. He thinks it is he who is saving me.

I walk out my apartment door and head toward the stairwell, my feet clattering on the tiled floors.

Something inside me jerks, and it feels like a surge of cold air slicing through me.

I stand at the top of the first flight, twelve steep faience-covered steps. I look down at the shining lobby floor.

I can't say there is even a thought.

I can't say I pause at all, somehow knowing I can't.

The second my heel hits the top of the stair, I swivel it around and twist my body as hard as I can, my hip hitting the railing and my body rising and then crashing and then

How like the astonishing leaps my brother and I used to take off the warped and quivering dock at our grandparents' house. Leap after leap into the sludge-thick water. It was easy, as true and as ancient as anything I'd ever known.

By the time I limp back up the stairs to my apartment, a throbbing wound is hanging heavily over my right eye. My ankle is swelling neatly. The sharper pain in my chest makes me think I probably cracked a rib or two.

I make it to my living room. My head growing foggier, my stomach pitching with nausea, in a flash I am no longer upright.

By the time he arrives, like some Wild West sheriff storming through my door, my head feels strangely suspended, refusing my body entirely.

I can barely feel his hands on me when he lifts my head off the floor and slides a pillow underneath. He is careful not to move me. Even in his rage, his gorgeous, frustrated rage that nearly terrifies, he knows what to do and not do. Or he's remembering.

The sounds from his mouth fade in and out. '... did this to you... I knew ... I knew ... what happened ... can't you tell me ... doctor ... hospital...'

And then, as he winds down, as the ambulance comes and as he curls up beside me before they place me on the gurney, grave whispers, breath on my ear, heart pressed against my chest, sighing promises, and I know I have him.

I am in the hospital for three days with bruised ribs and a concussion and a sprained ankle. How could I know my brother would go to Mike Standish and break his jaw, two teeth, and his own hand in doing so?

Mike took the beating and kept his mouth shut. That is what Mike does.

When urged to press charges, I merely turn my head to the side and look away. In this way, I never have to tell another story.

Within a week, we are home. Bill moves my things into his house and closes out my lease. He tells me he has filed a missing person's report for Alice King née Steele, who apparently has left town.

I listen to his lies, all of them, with sympathetic eyes. Bill tells me he has found out that Alice bought a ticket to South America. That she planned to leave him. But that she never showed up on the ship's passenger list, so she could be anywhere.

'Are you going to try to find her? Take a leave of absence?'

His expression stiffens, in his eyes something distant and unbearably close at once. 'No. No, she'll come home when she's ready.'

'Of course she will,' I say, pouring him his morning cup of coffee.

His eyes float over to the window above the sink, as if she might suddenly appear there.

What is he thinking happened? That she, feeling abandoned by him when he didn't show up at the dock, has disappeared as a way of punishing him?

He never says a word about the telegram I

sent in her name (Darling – I couldn't bring this upon you too. Stop. It's better this way. Stop. I can start over and you can go on. Stop. I love you. Stop. Alice. Stop.).

I like to think that somehow he knew everything I had done, knew and understood. That this is ultimately, secretly what he wanted, too. He is free now, free of everything she brought and everything she drew out in him.

I hate to think that we can never speak of it, that both of us hold and will continue to hold and hold secrets so dark that to ask questions of the other might risk contaminating everything.

But standing there beside him as he waits for me to finish filling his coffee cup, standing there in the sun-drenched kitchen so white it glows, I feel that in an instant everything can be erased, that we are, in a quick breath, born anew and time has disintegrated and then rebuilt itself and a new world has formed that is the same as the old, the world before the accident, that awful collision and everything it brought.

I have one last, strained phone conversation with Mike Standish. He is gentlemanly about the jaw and the split teeth. And he says he won't ask me any questions about it.

'I guess I don't want to know, King. I imagine you're probably glad that Alice split.'

'It's been very hard for my brother.'

'I'm sure it has. But, you know, I bet you're taking awfully good care of him.'

'I'm trying to,' I say, ignoring something strange in his tone.

'So is this it? You're through with me?'

'Aren't you through with me?' I say.

He pauses briefly, as if deciding.

Then, 'I don't know, King. Last night I read a book. What do you make of that?'

I feel something knock loose inside me, I feel his face in front of me, eyes on me and silky hands warmer than they should be, than they have any right to be.

'Your world ... it's so dirty,' I whisper, as if to him in the dark, as if to myself. 'How do you live in it?'

I hear him laugh softly to himself, and in that laugh are things that are tender and things that are harder, meaner, truer. It is both at once. Always both at once.

'Lora,' he says. 'One last thing.'

'What?'

'Didn't you ever think that maybe I was just trying to protect you?'

'From what?' I shot back.

'Never mind. Never mind.' His voice trails off, and then I hear the receiver click. I hear it click over and over again. I think I held the phone in my hand, pressed to my ear, forever.

The letter is forwarded to me from my old address. It is postmarked the very day the ship was to leave dock. She must have mailed it on her way to meet my brother. I read it three times very fast and then I tear it up and then

Listen, Lora, when I told you what happened with Lois, it wasn't to boast and it wasn't to come clean, to confess. I told you because I wanted you to see. It was time for you to see.

You never trusted me, not once. How could you, given what your brother is? Who could be good enough, special enough, worthy enough, righteous enough for a man like your brother? God, he could make me shudder long after no man could make me shudder.

I guess I can tell you now: I started working you right away. I knew what I was up against. I was careful how dark my lipstick was, how low I'd wear my neckline, how I hung the drapes, made his dinner, danced with him at parties, and looked at him across rooms, across oceans, across crowded cocktail parties. I was beyond reproach.

But then I saw that you liked my dark edges. Here was the surprise long after anyone could surprise me. You liked it.

You liked the voile nightgown you saw in my closet, touched it with your milky fingers and asked me where I'd gotten it. When I bought you one of your own, your face steamed baby pink, but you wore it. I knew you'd wear it.

From there it was simple. I can't deny the kick I got out of putting you and Mike Standish together. The giddiness at the thought of you being wedged between the same corded elbows I was. *She'll never know he's such a bad lay,* Lois growled at me. *After me, he was better,* I said, not wanting to feel it, not wanting to enjoy it so. What would Bill... I turned hot with shame. I was obscene.

Of course, I had to be careful, had to watch. Was I letting you see too much? How far was too far? How much too much? Would I know?

Please understand. Trying to sleep all these nights; I'd lie in bed and think: There are things you can never tell these people. Things they can't hear. Things like what you will do if you have to, if your back is against the wall. Men you'll open your legs to. The open cashbox. Please. And if everything around you is runny and loose and awful, why shouldn't you take that hard shot of tight pleasure, that dusty tablet, that loaded bottle? A little inoculation, ward off the stained mattress, the time clock, the mother feeding you rancid mush?

How could I tell you and your brother any of that? Always huddled together, all flax and Main Street parades, pressed against each other on the patio steps, always so absorbed, so caught up in your own blood-closeness that you can't believe anything – anyone – else exists. Oh, there's a lot to be told about that. And then there was me, this damaged thing.

The things you can't tell – well, most of all, it's this: *The hardest thing in this world is finding out what you're capable of.*

My hands in your yellow hair, helping you get ready for a party, every party, I felt this was a sister, my sister, and I loved you, even your terrible judgment (on me, no less!) and, still more, your own terrible weakness. When I touched you, dug my fingers into your hair, it was as though you were a part of him, even smelled like him, all great plains, fresh grass and prairie. Because he was mine, so were you.

And so we shared everything, didn't we?

The main thing, darling: When you get this, your brother and I will be gone. It's best this way even if you can't see it. Try to understand. You must know you can't possibly give him what I can. And you know damn well why.

I won't say what I want to because you won't believe me. You can't see it and wouldn't see it. Not even when I showed it to you.

I guess I understand because maybe I wish

I didn't see everything, all the time. Even now, writing this, I can see your flat gray eyes. They're his.

Alice

Several weeks later, I drive to the Los Angeles Public Library and spend the day scouring newspapers from the previous month, crime beat stories in newspapers throughout the area.

Stories of mutilated starlets, scorched bodies, pregnant suicides, lost girls leaping, falling, and being pushed, strangled, shot, stabbed, and set in flames. All of them somehow in flames.

When I have nearly given up, my eyes catch a small headline in the Santa Ana *Register*. It reads, UNIDENTIFIED WOMAN FOUND DEAD IN RAVINE.

The article notes that the woman's body was virtually unrecognizable from having lain in several inches of standing water for so long. The only clue to her identity was a small card, an identification card of some sort, with the text nearly completely effaced by the water. All that remained were the letters Lo.

Lo

The irony is so rich as to be painful. Whose

identity – Lois, Lora, Lora, Lois – had Alice planned to wear, and did it matter?

her face faded away, erased by water, cold and dark and

I can see them both down there, one face wiped clean, made new, and one split apart, turned inside out. If I could, I'd give them back their faces, like in the solemn, lurid photograph lying on the carpet, the photograph that gives them tawdry life still, their twin faces turning out to face, always turning out to face me and say

Months before, before everything, this...

It was at Calisto's, after two hours of side-cars at a tiny table in the corner, Mike Standish with one arm around each of us, king of the castle, smoking and laughing.

Alice and I standing side by side in front of the mirror in the powder room, packed with primping women, music scattering through the door with each entrance and exit.

Suddenly, as she stained her lips hot red, Alice seemed struck by our matching images. She stopped and watched, as if transfixed. Then:

'Do you ever feel like you're being followed?' It was a bullet shot in my ear.

'What? What?' I said, tucking a stray strand of hair behind my ear and then tucking it again as it slid out, and then again once more.

She stopped and smiled dreamily, ashamedly. 'I'm sorry. I'm drunk, Lora. So drunk.'

'What? But what did you say?' I said, standing straight.

She looked around at all the preening women. 'Come on,' she said, scooping my arm in hers and pulling me out into the hallway, and down past a clanging kitchen toward the open door to a back alley.

'Alice, I...'

'It's okay. You don't have to pretend with me.'

'Pretend what?'

'That you don't like it. All of it and more still. Darker still.'

'I never think about it,' I said, even as I didn't know what she meant, or what I meant. 'I don't like it. I never thought about it once.'

She put her face close up to mine, peering hard at me. Heavy and confused with liquor, I thought she might somehow be able to know, to read my thoughts by staring hard enough, to know things about me I didn't even know.

'You don't have to talk about it, but it's something we both have, Lora. It's something we've both got in us.' She rapped her chest, her décolletage, glaring at me.

'I don't have it in me,' I found myself saying with sudden fierceness as the music swung mightily around us, pouring out loudly from the club, kicking up suddenly with the tempo, and the crowd swarming.

'I don't have it in me,' I said louder, trying to rise above the cacophony.

She said nothing but kept staring, her hand resting on her chest, her gaze unwavering.

'I don't have it in me.'

I don't have it in me.

I could feel my face contort, my voice rise and crack, fighting the band for all it was worth, fighting the street sounds streaming through from the alley, the clattering dishes from the kitchen, those hard eyes boring through me.

I don't have it in me.

Not at all.

The publishers hope that this book has given you enjoyable reading. Large Print Books are especially designed to be as easy to see and hold as possible. If you wish a complete list of our books please ask at your local library or write directly to:

Magna Large Print Books
Magna House, Long Preston,
Skipton, North Yorkshire.
BD23 4ND

This Large Print Book, for people
who cannot read normal print,
is published under the auspices of

THE ULVERSCROFT FOUNDATION